Blackness Interrupted:
Black Psychology Matters

NICÓL OSBORNE, MSW
TAMERA GITTENS, MHC

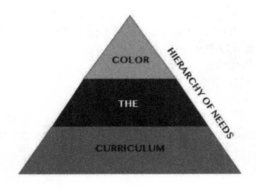

The Negative Space Publishing—Brooklyn, NY
ISBN: 978-0-578-88705-0
Library of Congress Control Number: 2021906883
Title: *Blackness Interrupted: Black Psychology Matters*
Author: Nicól Osborne, Tamera Gittens
Digital distribution | 2021
Paperback | 2021

Cover art illustrated and designed by Dennis Owusu-Ansah

Blackness Interrupted:
Black Psychology Matters

Dedication

This book is dedicated to anyone of African American descent, ranging from our ancestors to present-day African Americans and generations to come.

A special dedication to African Americans who have lost their lives and gone far too soon.

None of us should ever question our existence. African Americans are ordained for greatness.

Authors Note

It is imperative that when mentioning the history of psychology in America, we pay homage to the significant contributions made by African American professionals in the field. A conversation between Nicól and Tamera is the foundation of this book's creation. While looking for a psychology related gift, Nicól stumbled across a bag that contained photos of mental health professionals' . One of the professionals-was an African American woman. After some discussion with Tamera, they realized they knew very little about this person or her contributions to psychology. After some research, they learned not only was there limited research on this woman's background, but that she was Mamie Phipps Clark, an African American social psychologist who was one of the first African Americans to obtain doctorate degrees from Columbia University. Nicól and Tamera realized there was hardly any information on African American mental health providers.

This book discusses an issue-based assessment of the literature gap regarding African American contribution to psychology in America. Research has been collected on past and current African American psychologists and psychiatrists among other behavioral health clinicians in efforts to educate African Americans. Much can be said about limitations and lack of information regarding this topic. Thus, all data collected examines proposed changes to increase effectiveness and efficiency to rectify this diversity concern. We hope to help other African

American students and prospective mental health providers understand who paved the way for their successes.

Worldwide leadership has failed African Americans by glorifying Eurocentric culture and blatantly disregarding African American history. Some people may ask why a book full of African Americans, specifically Black psychologists/psychiatrists is necessary, and they are precisely the issue. We'd like those same people to understand that every culture is allowed to be acknowledged. We celebrate the ongoing battle of commemorating African American legacy, those that have endured pain but persisted and established new barriers sharing their extraordinary talent with the world. We recognize their phenomenal achievements in the field of mental health and will continue to help correct historical omissions. We want to amplify the worldwide demand for a fairer share of education, economic development, health, and wellness. We reaffirm our commitment to continue to invest in African Americans who are underserved, undervalued, and underprivileged regarding involuntary Whiteness.

Representation does matter and cultivates an understanding of racial identity, especially for African American descent children. The end goal is to educate those undergoing education by providing resources to make informed, comprehensive education decisions.

Epigraph

"Psychology is part of America, Black people are invisible in America, [and so] they're invisible in psychology. This invisibility, along with engrained expectations that Blacks were in general inferior to whites, was not based on data but culture – and therefore was hardly worthy of the name 'science.' You created a 'science' that reflects the belief of the society."

—*Joseph L. White*

"We don't have the luxury of being one dimensional... even though we are in a state of crisis, we don't act like it. We are very nonchalant about the fact that we are being targeted for extermination! I'm seeing Black folks more concerned with what they wear, more concerned with how they dress, more concerned with how expensive their car is, more concerned with the internet, more concerned with the shows on TV than I am about their existence. How do you explain the nonchalance in the face of danger? Post Traumatic Slavery Disorder. We have been socialized to be desensitized to our own dehumanization. We are the only people who can look at our own pain and trauma and neglect it. Not even neglect it, but laugh at it."

—*Dr. Umar Johnson*

"The failure to see color only benefits white America. A world without color is a world without racial debt."

—*Dr. Michael Eric Dyson*

Acknowledgments

No thanks to this persuasive loop of intergenerational traumatic injustice by the hands of racism. Not a drop of thankfulness can be offered in 2021 while having to advocate for equality, which should be an innate human right. Black pain is abstract and directly correlates to dismantling racist American systems.

Yet here we are, still.

Table of Contents

Preface

It goes without saying that from elementary school to doctorate studies, the curriculum taught is based on a Eurocentric perspective. Eurocentric curriculums do not challenge the dominant narrative or provide space for students of color to acknowledge people's achievements in history that look just like them. Psychology is no different as professors instruct students to complete assignments based on these curriculums. This loosely translates to ensuring students comprehend white psychology, amongst other white topics. African Americans are set up to contribute to white psychology research from the very beginning. Students are expected to demonstrate white history competency through standardized testing and other assignments, which results in a pass or fail. When research is utilized, there is a specific selection of textbooks chosen that accentuates white authors, and through search engines, many students are directed towards specific white psychologists. As you may imagine, this level of restriction propels students to stay on track with a limited amount of research while Black psychology is neglected. As a result, there are African American doctorate students who have studied psychology since undergraduate school and have never been taught about African American psychologists. The lack of exposure is a disservice to all and aids in the failure of contributions to Black psychology. Students' option to contribute to the field is taken off the table by involuntary whiteness, ultimately outlined throughout Eurocentric education institutions.

A simple google search, inputting "top psychologists," summarizes the constant disappointment as an African American, never seeing people who look like you on professional influential lists. As expected, one usually stumbles upon names such as Freud, Piaget, Erickson, James, Bandura, Pavlov, Skinner, Klein, Jung, Rogers, etc. Even after a thorough search, not one African American Psychologist appears. Perplexing because much of how and why psychology is such a diverse field of study is due to the astonishing work done on behalf of African American psychologists and psychiatrists. How can African American prospective student mental health providers contribute to Black psychology discipline advances when such prominent figures are omitted from simple google searches and "replicable" lists?

The surveys utilized to generate these lists of notable psychologists do not include any African Americans. Still, the accomplishments put forth in this book undoubtedly exemplify how significant their contribution to psychology is. Thus, when you google search top psychologists - it is no surprise that the ones you are taught in school (which are all white) appear again on the list because they are the most utilized. This perpetuates the cycle of whiteness, disregarding African Americans' strides throughout history, as inevitably, we believe society wants us to forget about them. African American psychologists deserve better; we need to create our own accurate lists, starting now.

Introduction

Have you ever thought that if African Americans knew more about their history, how that would aid in self-realization or the fulfillment of one's own potential? If African Americans knew all about the positive contributions made by those who look just like them, there would be even more role models to look up to. There is something magnificent surrounding representation and how that affects how groups of people see themselves and what they believe they can do for themselves and others. There's a reason African American history has been kept silent, aside from the fact that a lot has been lost due to slavery. The reason stems from why it was illegal for Black slaves to learn how to read and write. Knowing how to read and write made us powerful, just as knowing our history would. Although this book provides information on African American psychologists and psychiatrists specifically, challenge yourself to find out as much as possible about the African Americans that have contributed to your potential or current career field. That information will awaken the mind and reveal all the possibilities and potential you possess, despite your race or ethnicity.

Black psychology is compartmentalized within many topics centralized around African Americans. Throughout the chapters, we will provide ways that prospective African American mental health providers and the average person could educate themselves, learning conceptual frameworks for studying, understanding, contributing to Black psychology, and how the lack of knowing such is detrimental to the overall development of African Americans within society. Specifically, we will discuss the educational route of becoming a Psychologist/Psychiatrist, contributing to psychology as an African American, and examining Black psychology study's historical influences. Many of these historical influences are not taught in Psych 101 in college, and even as a Masters or Doctorate student, these names are still absent from lectures and textbooks. Even if you are not interested in psychology, learning more about these African Americans' history and how they influenced psychology is relevant. Much of what Black psychology is today has stemmed from these individuals' work. Many of the conversations around culturally sensitive techniques and practices today started because those individuals noticed the disparity of mental health services between Blacks and Whites. If many of us knew how much African Americans contributed to the field, maybe there would be a different outlook on the topic of mental health. This outlook is what deters many from seeking help and reinforces the stigma around mental health in the Black community.

A narrative concerning self-care, promoting Blackness and choosing a therapist as an African American is also discussed, which are not talked about enough. When it is mentioned, it is phrased as "you must" or "you have to" without tangible ways of actually going about the journeys of self-care, promoting Blackness, or even seeking therapy. We highlight the current status of

Black psychology. This includes but is not limited to a significant gap in the literature, the lack of acknowledgment within educational institutions amongst other notions that conclude Black psychology is not a legitimate field or discipline of psychology and the impact lack of representation may have on the aptitude of African Americans students. A critical analysis is reviewed, and the chapters end with a summary.

Chapter One

Outline: How to Become a Psychologist

1. Earn a Master's Degree - Preferably in Psychology, Social Work, Sociology or Mental Health Counseling. (Sometimes Bachelor Degree is Sufficient- Some States Allow Master Level Psychologists to practice).
2. Take The Graduate Record Examinations (GRE): If applicable.
3. Complete Ph.D. or PsyD.
4. Complete Clinical Hours: Practicum, Internship, and Postdoctoral Hours. (the State of Licensure Depends on which are Applicable & # of Hours Needed)
5. Take Examination For Professional Practice in Psychology (EPPP)
6. Jurisprudence Exam (If State of Licensure Requires)
7. Earn and Maintain Licensure

Outline: How to Become a Psychiatrist

1. Earn a Bachelor's Degree - Preferably in Pre Med, Physical Science or Psychology (Master's Degree Optional)
2. Take the Medical College Admissions Test (MCAT)
3. Complete M.D or D.O Program
4. Complete a Residency Program
5. Earn and Maintain License and Board Certification

Chapter Two

*Eurocentric Standardized Testing: Academic Achievement
Gap & Racial Hierarchy*

N ow that we have shared a synapse of becoming a
psychologist and psychiatrist, keep in mind that
the route from beginning to end is completely
centralized around whiteness. Eurocentric curriculum and
standardized testing work together to eliminate African
Americans' opportunities and support racist whites
directly.

Academically, not one step throughout becoming a
clinician does psychology touch upon Black psychology.
Eurocentric disciplines such as Psychology 101, History
of Psychology, Abnormal, Cognitive, Developmental,
Physiological, Experimental Statistics/Research, etc., are
all within the degree plan. Students are required to take
Ethics, but even with that, racism and healthcare
disparities aren't showcased within case studies. We are
not taught about a single African American psychologist,
psychiatrist, or Black psychology when obtaining
doctorate degrees.

Standardized testing equates to academic achievement
gaps and racial hierarchy, which are both racist and are
extremely detrimental to African Americans
psychologically. The standardized testing leading up to
being professionals reflects the whiteness learned
throughout the courses outlined above. This does not
mean that you cannot pass the exam if you are indeed

African American. Simply put, because these tests intentionally lack diversity, favoring Eurocentric culture and history, the lack of relatability naturally causes a disconnect.

African American students are expected to pass examinations centralized around this curriculum. White students are expected to be multiculturally competent clinicians by only learning 'white psychology' or the psychology that has been centralized around white people, their views, and culture. This can result in white privilege in white coats, which may indirectly lead to healthcare disparities. Racial bigotry is a huge issue in healthcare, and it stems from a lack of training and academic understanding reflected in coursework.

We are led to believe that these sorts of standardized exams reflect our self-worth. If one does not score well, it reflects our efforts, or worse, the belief that we do not understand psychology. Laughably, one is led to internalize that one examination has the ability to reflect intellectual levels of a diverse population measure within a "single, standardized weight scale." These beliefs cause African American test takers to think that they are lesser than or intellectually inferior. 'white psychology' was formulated through racist hypotheses, which suggest that African Americkans are beneath Whites. Like everything else in America, Whites may not legally exclude us, but they created alternative routes to oppress African Americans. These false feelings of inadequacy emerge from childhood. In actuality, higher-income neighborhoods suggest higher taxes. Higher taxes suggest that schools are well funded. Lower-income African Americans will attend schools that are not properly funded, which equates to not having enough textbooks. Students are greatly affected by the caliber of teachers hired down to the food served in the cafeteria. Therefore, these standardized tests that measure "intelligence" are not accurate based on the opportunities afforded to a white student from an upper-class neighborhood that is not endowed to a Black student who lives in a lower-income neighborhood.

Racist ideas are created out of differences in environments. As you'll learn when reading about Robert Lee Williams II, Ph.D., culture, and testing are important factors to explore and conclude that race cannot be ranked superior and inferior due to just that. Differences do not equate to inferiority. One cannot suggest that low-income African Americans testing lower than upper-class whites concludes that African Americans are inferior. Achievements should quantify intelligence; anything else suggests racism.

We must mitigate racism in psychology and healthcare by fusing current Eurocentric standardized testing with Black psychology and eliminating biased standardized testing in general. Dr. Michael Eric Dyson spoke on the commonwealth club, and the discussion was centralized around *"America's Unfinished Race Conversation."* Dr. Dyson articulated how we cannot conclude African American children are inferior in any capacity when their most updated textbooks show Roosevelt as the last president, which speaks volumes when examining how underfunded Black schools are.

Additionally, incorporating Black psychology into Eurocentric curriculums, diversifying academic coursework, resulting in a fairer opportunity for

African Americans, is necessary. Our education systems do not focus on expanding minds; instead, it's filled with involuntary whiteness and tested on how much is retained. Intellectual differences are not valued in 'white psychology,' standardized testing does not reflect multiculturalism or antiracists. Intellectual openness is not encouraged; instead, standardized testing is utilized to exemplify an efficient education system. Standardized testing coincides with racist hierarchy and the academic achievement gap.

Examination for Professional Practice in Psychology Statistics

The Examination for Professional Practice in Psychology (EPPP) is a requirement for psychology licensure within the United States of America. Limited but viable studies conclude that the EPPP discriminates against African Americans. What's enraging is that after all the extensive data that has been collected, cross-examined, and thoroughly summarized, nothing has been done to overturn this disadvantage. We simply are made aware of the unfairness. The tests have not been altered, nor have they been removed, declaring that African American needs are irrelevant regarding Eurocentric standardized examinations.

Usually, when a test has this level of significant impact, industrial psychologists investigate and carefully evaluate methods by researching more. The passage of the EPPP heavily influences professional ramifications for applicants. If it potentially causes African Americans barriers amongst other minorities, why hasn't anything been modified? While the Association of State and Provincial Psychology Boards (ASPPB) — the organization that prepares the EPPP; denied any discrimination, research suggests otherwise.

While America is set to turn majority non-white by 2045, lack of representation will be catastrophic for African Americans who have mental health issues and need care. According to the journal *Psychiatric Services*, Ethnic minorities are more likely to experience risk factors such as poverty and poor health that ultimately spark mental health issues. Yet, only 1 in 3 African Americans who need mental health care receives it. America needs African American therapists when this ticking time bomb goes off.

The ASPPB states they are open to criticism but do nothing with the feedback. The ASPPB recently began analyzing data on candidates' racial and ethnic backgrounds to compare individual questions' performance within the exam. The question remains, why is that necessary if the test is apparently "unbiased?"

This is just another standardized test that explores if the applicant is a successful test taker, not if that person will be a competent psychologist. Successful test takers are not likely to reflect those that are racially underrepresented, all of which stem from economic disadvantages. The EPPP has no limit on how many times you take the test. Still, statistically, not many African American families can afford a roughly $700 exam, not including the study material expenses. In January 2020, the ASPPB launched a second part of the EPPP, and while it is a separate entity, it is an addition to the already controversial exam.

Much needs to be done to regain African Americans' trust concerning standardized testing, specifically with the ASPPB and EPPP. While some whites may denounce the passing rate to African Americans not being prepared to take exams, this is very much the result of systemic racism, yet again.

Susan Andrews Ph.D. wrote an article in 2018, *"New Study Shows EPPP Can Discriminate Against African-Americans, Hispanics."* This article discusses that the difference between Whites and African Americans/Hispanics is so large that minorities fall into "disparate impact" discrimination, as described in Title VII of the Civil Rights Act of 1964.

Brian Sharpless, Ph.D. wrote an article in 2018, *" Are demographic Variables Associated with Performance on the Examination for Professional Practice in Psychology (EPPP)?"* This article demonstrated numerical findings related to the lack of Black/Hispanic psychologists. He found that Blacks had a failure rate of 38.50%, and Hispanics had a failure rate of 35.60%. Whereas Whites had a failure rate of 14.07%, and Asians had a failure rate of 24%. Brian Sharpless concluded that the failure rate for Black and Hispanic EPPP applicants in the state was 2.5 times the rate for white applicants in the period up to 2017.

Molly Fosco wrote an article in 2019, *" MENTAL DIVIDE: THE PSYCHOLOGY TEST THAT'S FAILING MINORITIES"* This article showcased that the odds are loaded against psychologists of color — starting with the professional licensing examination

— even if they hold top degrees. With the EPPP, non-white test-takers are twice as likely to fail to qualify as psychologists despite holding doctoral degrees, according to a previously unreported 2018 survey by the American Psychological Association (APA).

EPPP Question Example

Q1: During your initial session with your client, you learn that their history of offenses is difficult for you to deal with; therefore, you do not want to work with your client. As an ethical psychologist, you should:
- **A. Disregard your feelings and work with your client.**
- **B. Refer your client to another Psychologist**
- **C. Accept the new client but speak about this case during supervision.**
- **D. Tell the new client you cannot see them for therapy.**

While B is the answer, the African American test taker might have grown up in environments knowing many people who have offenses, and it may not bother them. They may not identify ALL offenses as bad, culturally.

Outside of that, how does referring your client to someone who also may not have the same ideologies ingrained in them help the client? This would create a recurring cycle where psychologists do not feel comfortable with clients and histories of offenses. Hence, African Americans are less likely to undergo **therapeutic sessions with non-Black clinicians due to a lack of relatability.**

Q2: During the past few sessions, an 18-year-old client has become progressively depressed and threatens suicide. They express feeling unhappy with therapy progress and state that they will not return. What is the best course of action for the Psychologist:

    A. Get the involuntary commitment of the client immediately.

    B. Encourage the client to continue therapy and try to obtain a "no suicide contract."

    C. Call the family immediately to discuss the situation.

    D. Recognize that the client has the right to self-determination, terminating therapy.

While B is the answer, the African American test taker could have chosen to alert the clients' family since therapists are allowed to break doctor/patient confidentiality if clients harm themselves or others.

Medical College Admission Test Statistics

The Medical College Admission Test (MCAT) is a mandated competency evaluation utilized as a prerequisite before being accepted into medical school within the United States of America. White males have always dominated the medical field, but as America transitions into a more ethnically saturated society, ironically, the profession remains unchanged. The common denominator is the MCAT.

In 1986, John Hopkins momentarily discontinued utilizing the MCAT to encourage and empower diverse applicants. Studies have shown that the notion was correct and influential concerning getting minorities to apply. A study published with *Higher Education* during 2016 concluded that qualified Blacks were prevented from entering medical school due to the gap between themselves and whites through the examination.

Much like the EPPP, the MCAT can largely be influenced by the test takers' background. In a study published in *Academic Medicine: the Journal of the Association of American Medical Colleges* (AAMC) in May 2013, African American and Latino test-takers' average MCAT scores were lower than white examiners. While articles do not always shed light on test bias, they highlight that cultural factors are a potential reason for the gap within performances.

As we discuss the EPPP and lack of representation, there seems to be the same problem with the MCAT. The same issue is summarized, concluding that there is a lack of diversity due to admission policies. Ultimately, a lack of ethnic diversity affects patients. White clinicians do not normally come from areas where patients are underserved. The lack of African American Psychiatrists causes patients to wait longer for care because relatability is comforting.

Hopefully, America will rethink their approach to admission protocols. The academic achievement gap's impact is not worth keeping the MCAT mandatory for Medical school. Under-represented African Americans should have the opportunity to give back to their community and contribute to the field of medicine, specifically Black psychiatry.

Black Experiences Effect on
Higher Education

Black students are constantly in contact with racism's emotional pervasive cycle. The demands of educational excellence coupled with operating through uninviting hallways, exposure to outright verbal racial slurs or physical assault is distracting, to say the least. It may feel like Black students have to additionally combat school racism as if it is a part-time job, while all of this may lead to burn out due to daily heightened feelings and emotions. Ultimately, this is unhealthy and can lead to poor overall health outcomes and possible unsatisfactory academic outcomes.

If asked, more times than often, Black students will express how normalized microaggression circumstances within schools are and how many of those times schools turn a blind eye or outright do not address those issues. Racial incidents are prevalent in predominantly white schools, and Black students are consistently subjected to deep-rooted prejudices by white teachers and students. This causes Black students to feel displaced and hyperaware, and distrusting of Whiteness. None of this changes from pre-k through obtaining one's doctorate degree.

Many teachers do not hold themselves accountable for being multiculturally competent or acknowledging and celebrating Black students' humanity. Oftentimes, they do not push the envelope. That lack of effort, concern, and urgency is critical to Black student outcomes. The few Black faculty members that students have available to them are sanctuaries. There is a positive correlation between hiring more Black instructors and better educational outcomes for Black students. Black students who have one Black teacher by third grade are 7% more likely to graduate high school and 13% more likely to enroll in college (Perry, 2019). After having two Black teachers, Black students' likelihood of enrolling in college increases by 32% (Perry,2019). Systemic racism cannot be rectified without hiring Black teachers, but this would require Black instructors to trust institutions that refuse to dismantle Eurocentric education reforms.

It is no surprise that in the U.S., only 2,000 of the estimated 28,000 psychiatrists are Black, and the total number of psychiatrists is rapidly decreasing since three out of five psychiatrists are over 55-years-old. *(HeartandSoul, 2019)*. When we remember how many unhealthy frequent racist predicaments Blacks have had to experience from the onset of beginning school, unfortunately, it makes sense. Throughout elementary school, Black history month is confined to a month; rather than all year long and still extremely limiting. Black students can name at least one time a Black instructor has asked them to teach the classroom about the Black experience in middle school. In high school, Black students can admit that they have thought about leaving school altogether, at least once. In college, Black students reveal that white college administrators merely seem to be "woke," but still, you feel voiceless.

According to a 2015 report, there are more than 43,000 school resource officers and other sworn police officers, and an additional 39,000 security guards, working in the nation's 84,000 public schools

(National Center for Education Statistics, 2015). It is particularly troubling that law enforcement is so often called in to discipline Black students on school grounds. When a simple altercation at school leads to an arrest for assault, something has gone terribly wrong. This phenomenon is known as the School to Prison Pipeline because it's channeling students right into the criminal justice system, where people of color can expect unfair treatment.

Clinicians have conducted many studies that explain how addressing educational racism is beneficial in terms of African Americans' mental health. We must ask ourselves why the United States is suffering from a dramatic shortage of psychiatrists and other mental health providers. The shortfall is particularly dire in rural regions, urban neighborhoods, and community mental health centers that often treat the most severe mental illnesses. (*AAMC*,2018). Most importantly, what are we going to do about it? If we do not properly create spaces to encourage Blackness when Black students are young, they will not aspire to become more. They will succumb to societal barriers and negative psychological thoughts believing they can't be more no matter how hard they work, by virtue of being Black.

Zero tolerance policy implementation needs to be put in place effective immediately. Change needs to be taken seriously to address questions, comments, and concerns that Black students have. All of such should be directed to the highest entity of that educational institution. Acknowledging the trials and tribulations of the hurt and pain that Black students have had to operate through is not enough.

Discussions of systemic and institutional racism need to happen as much as racial incidents occur against Black students.

Chapter Three
*Disciplines of Psychology: What is Black Psychology'?
Why is it not acknowledged?*

African Americans have not been properly serviced in the mental health system. Explanations for African American disparities in mental health services are instilled in adverse factors such as biases when assessing mental health needs, access to mental health services, variations in treatment facilities, interpersonal and institutional racism.

Anything that has deviated from the white/Eurocentric view was usually met with disapproval, skepticism, and doubt throughout history. This disapproval also holds for the term used profoundly today amongst African American psychologists and many in the mental health field called Black psychology. Like multicultural counseling, Black psychology focuses solely on African Americans' experience emphasizing worldview and all that encompasses. The value system, traditions, spirituality, sexuality, relationships, and social context of African Americans are critical when conceptualizing the African American experience and then using these components to create racially and culturally sensitive treatment models. There are many Black life expressions beyond what is associated with African Americans. There has always been ambiguity regarding the term "African American" and "Black." However, African American refers to ethnicity, and Black refers to race, but in national estimates, Caribbean and African immigrants have been included in African American populations. In therapy, the importance of learning this information is knowing whether a client identifies more as Black or African American, which is salient when forming their concerns and can be a direct therapeutic intervention. Both race and ethnicity verbiage will be used throughout the book, as we refer to some general experiences of being Black in America.

The arguments have been presented that the same applications that can be used to counsel white Americans can be used for counseling African Americans, as we all present with similar developmental milestone struggles, but this is simply not true. African Americans' struggles can be traced back 400 years ago from slavery through segregation to continued individual, cultural and institutional racism. Standard psychology has never focused on the oppression that African Americans have faced and continue to face, and it certainly has not focused on the direct effects of racism. Every treatment model has been based on the dominant white culture's worldview. As we try to move towards a more culturally sensitive and inclusive treatment model for African Americans in the mental health field, Black psychology is that driving force. More than ever, this change is needed. Many African Americans may only seek help when they believe to be suffering from severe mental health issues and not what they perceive to be minor issues, which they may still need help navigating. This is the outcome of a lack of trust in the mental health care system. Mistrust stems from perceived and accurate negative characteristics of mental health services, but cultural mistrust also seems to be another factor that aids in the apprehension.

Many of the influential African American psychologists mentioned in this book are noteworthy. Black psychology needs to be acknowledged and understood, as African Americans' experience is still drastically different from any other race today. Issues of race should always have a space in therapy when needed. Race has been a central part of lived experiences for many African Americans. African Americans often come into treatment with the weight of historical inequality and experiences of racism and discrimination on their shoulders, so it is a disservice to the client when a counselor cannot talk about diversity issues in therapy. Black Lives Matter is the slogan formulated against police brutality that has taken the lives of many, such as Breonna Taylor, George Floyd, Philando Castille, and so many more. African Americans must live through this blatant racism and still function through society seamlessly. Mental health care providers must understand the African American client and use culturally sensitive therapy tools.

Chapter Four
Statistics

According to the American Counseling Association, 86 percent of psychologists in the U.S. workforce are white, 5 percent are Asian, 5 percent are Hispanic, 4 percent are Black/African American, and 1 percent are multiracial or from other racial/ethnic groups. African Americans make up 13 percent of the United States population but only 2 percent are psychiatrists. This is less diverse than the U.S. population, which consist of 62 percent white, and 38 percent racial/ethnic minority (APA, 2020).

The lack of African American psychologists is not due to disinterest but rather a lack of information that stems from misconceptions and cultural stigma. African Americans with mental conditions have a more challenging time recovering because healthcare systems lack cultural competency and social stigma. The overall process causes a discrepancy. This is why having a mental health provider who is relatable with patient experience and identity is critical regarding the road of recovery. Outside of the overall health concern, educationally, this image of representation shows that aspirations are obtainable despite being African American.

When referencing the mistrust that African Americans have in America's healthcare system, the information that studies provide contains substantial reasons. Studies show African Americans are just as much at risk for mental illness as their white counterparts yet receive drastically less treatment. African Americans often receive poorer care quality and lack access to culturally competent care. Only one-in-three African Americans who need mental health care received it. (APA, 2017). In 2018, 58.2 percent of Black and African American young adults 18-25 and 50.1 percent of adults 26-49 with serious mental illness did not receive treatment. Nearly 90 percent of Black and African American people over the age of 12 with a substance use disorder did not receive treatment (Mental Health America, 2020).

Black and African American people are more often diagnosed with schizophrenia and less often diagnosed with mood disorders than white people with the same symptoms (APA, 2017). Part of the reason for this can be found as a result of the differences in how African Americans express symptoms of emotional distress, which may contribute to misdiagnosis. Multicultural Counseling is emerging as part of every counseling degree to help students understand that they will have clients from different cultures that may explain their symptoms and talk about their problems "differently" from what the Diagnostic Statistical Manual may include. For example, African Americans may explain that they have been experiencing aches when talking about depression. Although this information is emerging, as statistics show, African Americans are still not receiving the care they need from culturally competent professionals. Ultimately, there is a huge need for African American professionals in the mental health field.

Compared with whites, African Americans are:

- **Less likely to receive guideline-consistent care:** *While the implementation of the Affordable Care Act has helped to close the gap in uninsured individuals, 11.5 percent of Black and African Americans, versus 7.5 percent of white Americans were still uninsured in 2018 (Kaiser Family Foundation, 2020).*
- **Less frequently included in the research:** *When African Americans are not included in the research, the studies that are being done are concluded based on the dominant white participants. Those conclusions will not work in therapy with African Americans.*
- **More likely to use emergency rooms or primary care (rather than mental health specialists):** *There is a stigma within the African American community that if a mental health facility is sought, that means the person has a serious mental illness. They may believe that having a mental illness is a weakness, and they may be ostracized from the community if that is shared. There is a lack of education regarding mental health and how mental health professionals can assist. Therapy is not only for people who have serious mental illnesses but also for those who would like someone to talk to for everyday*

problems and can assist people in becoming a better version of themselves, as they see fit. Many African Americans may also believe that counselors will not understand them because of the lack of diversity in the mental health field.

- **More likely to be incarcerated than people of other races with mental health conditions, particularly with schizophrenia, bipolar disorders, and other psychoses**: *It goes without saying that many police officers are not trained to handle people that have mental illnesses and when they do receive calls with these issues, what usually happens is the person with the mental illness gets incarcerated when they do not cooperate. Black and African American people make up 13 percent of the general U.S. population but nearly 40 percent of the prison population. In 2016, the imprisonment rate for Black and African American men (2,417 per 100,000 Black male residents) was more than 6 times greater than that for white men (401 per 100,000 white male residents). The imprisonment rate for Black and African American women (97 per 100,000 Black and African American female residents) was almost double that for white women (49 per 100,000 white female residents) (Mental Health America, 2020). Additionally, many of these people may be homeless or live below the poverty line without proper care access. About 27% of African Americans live below* *the poverty level compared to about 10.8% of non-Hispanic whites (APA, 2017).*

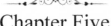

Chapter Five
Solomon Carter Fuller (1897)
First African American Psychiatrist

We have to acknowledge the determination and tenacity it takes to become the first African American psychiatrist in the United States when racial inequality and discrimination were a crippling staple of society for African Americans at that time. The number of trials and tribulations that Fuller faced was significant, but he continued to prevail with groundbreaking research and contributions to the health and mental health field. Fuller was born in 1872 in Monrovia, Liberia. Fuller was a direct descendant of slavery; his grandfather was a Virginia slave who bought his family's freedom then relocated to Norfolk, Virginia. Fuller was always interested in medicine from a young age, especially since his grandparents were medical missionaries who supported his dreams. At the age of 17, Fuller left Liberia for America and attended Livingstone College in North Carolina, graduating with his Bachelor's degree in 1893. Fuller then attended Long Island College Medical School and completed his medical degree at the Boston University School of Medicine in 1897. Fuller completed his internship at Westborough State Hospital in Boston, working as a pathologist.

Afterward, he became a professor at the Boston University School of Medicine.

Fuller faced discrimination within the medical field throughout his employment, ranging from unequal salaries and underemployment. Most of his work included autopsies, which was not normal during that era. While conducting autopsies, Fuller discovered many scientific findings that allowed his career to advance while contributing to the medical communities, which once shunned him.

Fuller did a lot of his work centralized around degenerative diseases of the brain and majorly contributed to Alzheimer's disease. Fuller's post-graduate studies included pathology and neuropathology specifically. In 1903, Fuller was one of five specially selected clinicians chosen by Alois Alzheimer to research at the Royal Psychiatric Hospital at Munich University. Fuller helped teach fellow clinicians how to properly assess and diagnose the effects of syphilis, which helped prevent Black war veterans from being misdiagnosed, discharged, and ineligible for military benefits due to side effects. Fuller was the main trainer of young doctors at the Veterans Hospital in Tuskegee, Alabama, before the unfortunately infamous Tuskegee Syphilis Experiments (1932-1972).

In 1905, Fuller returned to Westborough Hospital and continued his role as a neuropathologist and founded the "Westborough State Hospital Papers" which published local research activity. His interest in Alzheimer's disease led him to become a leading authority in the subject. In 1912, Fuller published a profound piece, the first comprehensive review of

Alzheimer's disease, and reviewed eleven known cases. He was also known for describing the ninth recorded case of the disease. In 1907, Fuller published a case series describing the neuropathological features of patients diagnosed with conditions that included "dementia paralytica" and "dementia denilis." Four years later, Fuller questioned the importance of plaques and neurofibrillary pathology as hallmarks of Alzheimer's disease.

In 1919, Fuller resigned from Westborough Hospital and decided to pursue medical education full time at Boston University. He became the associate professor of neuropathology and later became the neurology associate professor. Despite these significant titles and being the only African American on the faculty, he was not acknowledged on payroll and made significantly less than his fellow white professors. From 1928 to 1933, he acted as chair of the Department of Neurology, even though he was not actually given the title. His retirement came in 1933 when a junior white assistant professor was promoted to professor and appointed the official department chair despite the work Fuller did for those many years. Fuller once said, "With the sort of work that I have done, I might have gone farther and reached a higher plane had it not been for the color of my skin."

After his retirement, Fuller was given the title of emeritus professor of neurology at Boston University. However, he continued to practice neurology and psychiatry in Massachusetts and for a period in Pennsylvania. The foundation of Fuller's career is rooted in teaching. Fuller started as a Professor but taught and continues to teach all African American clinicians how to be selfless truly but also a philanthropist. It is no surprise that someone of his personality would be the First African American psychiatrist. His contributions to the field and Black community are profound, especially regarding the Tuskegee Experiments. We must understand Tuskegee Experiments' history can not be explained without Dr. Fuller.

In 1974, The Black Psychiatrists of America created the Solomon Carter Fuller Program for young Black aspiring psychiatrists to complete their residency. The Solomon Carter Fuller Mental Health Center in Boston is also named after Dr. Fuller.

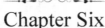

Chapter Six
Francis Sumner (1920)
First African American Psychologist

When acknowledging the accomplishments of Francis Sumner, it is noteworthy that not only was he the first African American Psychologist, but he also played a momentous and symbolic role in the education of early generations of Black psychologists that would come after him. Sumner's most noteworthy Master's student Kenneth Clark, would often cite Sumner and conclude that he was a major inspiration for his career as a social psychologist civil rights campaigner. Sumner is nicknamed the father of Black psychology, but not one of psychology's founding fathers. He is not mentioned throughout programs of study but undoubtedly plays a large role in the "Negro Education."

Sumner was born in Arkansas in 1895. His parents changed their surname to Sumner to honor Massachusetts's anti-slavery senator Charles Sumner whose primary focus was on the poor quality of segregated education. Sumner attended primary schools located in Virginia and New Jersey. Despite his extreme underprivileged upbringing, Sumner charged through obstacles as a Black male during his time. As the high schools were so inferior, Sumner did not attend, and his father home-schooled him, as his father was also self-taught. In 1911, with his father's assistance, Sumner passed the entrance examination to enter Lincoln University at 15 years old. Excelling academically, naturally, he showcased his intelligence by graduating as valedictorian and with honors in English, Greek, Latin, modern foreign languages, and philosophy. In 1916, with the encouragement from G. Stanley Clark, President of Clark College and University, Sumner transferred to Clark University to complete a second Bachelor's in English. Soon thereafter, Sumner went back to Lincoln University, and while teaching German and psychology, Sumner earned the M.A. degree in 1917.

Previously in 1909, Clark University conducted a landmark conference that housed 175 psychologists worldwide, including Freud and Jung. Whilst at Clark, Sumner cultivated a mentorship with G. Stanley Hall, who organized that conference. Hall was the first president of the American Psychological Association (APA), and in 1917, Hall approved Sumner's application for a Ph.D. in psychology. Sumner was briefly a military drafter, but on June 14, 1920, Francis Sumner acquired his Ph.D. in psychology at Clark University. His dissertation was on "Psychoanalysis of Freud and Adler." Following graduation, he began teaching at Clark University and then Wilberforce University, ending his teaching career at West Virginia. However, he continued to teach at various Black universities throughout his career. As a professor, Sumner published many Educational Review articles throughout his time. The publications were recognized as controversial since they were closely related to Booker T. Washington and the fundamentalist reforms of equality concerning higher education for African Americans. Sumner focused on addressing Black students' discriminatory treatment and the inferior standard of education. Sumner would later fail to secure funding to continue education surrounding his interest topic, which he previously noted as a lack of support for Black research. Thus, in 1940 the Southern Society for Philosophy and Psychology (SSPP) modified their rules to exclude Sumner deeming him ineligible for membership. Instead, Sumner became chair at the Howard University Psychology Department. He is also credited for separating the department of psychology from philosophy in 1930 when he became head of the department. Finally, he was an official abstractor for Psychological Bulletin and the Journal of Social Psychology and provided abstracts for more than 3,000 articles from German, French, and Spanish authors.

Chapter Seven
Albert Sydney Beckham (1930) & Ruth Howard (1934)
*First African American School Psychologist & First
African American Woman Psychologist*

School Psychology has a separate history within Psychology itself, and usually, there is no mention of African American contributors. When looking in certain history textbooks related to School Psychology such as *School Psychology Past, Present, and Future* or the *Encyclopedia of School Psychology,* one may think that these readings should be accurate as it tells the history of all the people that made great strides in the field. However, that is not the case, which brings us to Albert Sydney Beckham. Albert Sydney Beckham was the first African American School Psychologist and made great strides providing psychoeducational services to children under Chicago's Board of Education.

Albert Sydney Beckham was born in 1897 in Camden, South Carolina. He enrolled in Lincoln University at the age of 15 and graduated with his Bachelor's Degree in Psychology. One of his classmates at Lincoln was Francis Sumner, who we acknowledge as the first African American Psychologist. After Lincoln University, Albert enrolled in Ohio State University and received a second Bachelor's Degree and Master's Degree in Psychology. He moved to New York, and while attending New York University, he worked as an educator in New York's public school system. It was there where he began to gain an interest in children and possibly sparked his interest to pursue his doctorate with a specialty in children. He was offered a position to teach at Howard University. He created the first psychological laboratory at an African American institution and taught all psychology courses. Beckham assessed many African American children using many culturally sensitive techniques, such as establishing rapport when white psychologists published reports on intelligence levels of different ethnic groups but were not aware of the test's biases or culturally appropriate procedures. Beckham provided intelligence testing, individual counseling, and consultation services within Washington D.C's school districts.

After working at Howard University for five years, Beckham pursued his doctorate at New York University and wrote his dissertation on "A Study of the Intelligence of Colored Adolescents of Different Socioeconomic Status in Typical Metropolitan Areas." After graduation, Beckham worked at the Institute for Juvenile Research, the first child guidance clinic in the United States that dealt with only childhood disorders. During his time here, the Great Depression affected his pay greatly, and when changing careers, he decided to take the psychologist examination for Chicago Public Schools. He passed but was not appointed a position until the National Urban League pressured the board, and he was reluctantly given a position cooped with the words "Go to DuSable High School and work for your people." Beckham worked as a School Psychologist for Chicago Public Schools and established one of the first psychological school clinics in DuSable High School. During his time at the high school, he published 21 articles that included topics such as intelligence testing, childhood behaviors, and the effects of counseling high school students.

In the famous 1971 case of Larry P. v. Riles, San Francisco Unified School District filed suit in the Federal District Court of Northern California, stating that five African American students were placed in special education based on racially intelligence testing biased and discriminatory. Intelligence testing used to place African American children in special education was deemed illegal in California. During Beckham's time period, the fact that African Americans were disproportionately put into special education prompted Beckham to bring awareness to the issue through his publications. The topic of intelligence testing for African American children is an important one, as the issue still presents itself today. In 2016, 12 percent of Black children across the nation received services at school for disabilities ranging from emotional disturbances to physical disabilities to intellectual impairment. Only 8.5 percent of white children received those services. His focus on childhood behavior problems was seen through publications like "The Behavior Problem Clinic and the Negro Child," in which he described the increasing behavior problems in African American children. He concluded that children's social and environmental conditions at that time were the cause of these problems, and an early diagnosis could save children from getting a juvenile court record.

Influential in her own right, Dr. Ruth Howard, Beckham's wife, was either the first or second woman in the United States to receive her doctorate in psychology depending on the criteria. The criteria are based on the education department's degree versus the psychology department. Born on March 4th, 1900 in Washington D.C., Howard graduated from Columbia University with a Masters in Social Work. She later attended the University of Minnesota, where she received her Ph.D. in Psychology and Child Development in 1934. Focusing on child development, she studied the developmental history of 229 triplets for her doctoral research, which was thought to be a large study at the time. This research was published in the Journal of Psychology and the Journal of Genetic Psychology. Ruth Howard obtained a job as the Director of Mental Health and Training with the National Youth Administration. This program resulted from the Great Depression and was tasked to help the youth with job training and skills, so Howard was responsible for assessing the youth's work assignment and mastery of certain job skills. Along with this, Ruth Howard helped her husband Albert Beckham maintain their private practice, The Center for Psychological Services. Howard pursued postdoctoral studies at the University of Chicago, where she studied projective techniques with Robert Havinghurst, client-centered therapy with Carl Rogers, and play therapy with Virginia Axline. While working with Virginia Axline, Howard published her own study of play interviews with kindergarteners and 4th graders, focusing on the play interviews that could be used to detect war attitudes during World War II.

Chapter Eight
Inez Beverly Prosser (1933)
First African American Woman Psychologist

Inez Beverly Prosser was the first woman Black psychologist. During the early 20th century, she focused on educational psychology and the effects of racism, yet she is not spoken about throughout teachings, nor are her successes throughout educational institutions. Researchers are unsure of her birthday's exact year but conclude the month and day is December 30th, possibly 1895. During Prosser's time, there were limited educational opportunities for African Americans, so Prosser began a fund to help her ten siblings through high school and college. All of them graduated high school, but only five went onto college, including Prosser. Despite the upward battle of facing sexism and racism, she excelled academically throughout the school.

In 1912, Prosser was awarded a teaching certificate and continued to teach until 1927. Prosser received her Bachelor's degree shortly after and began her Master's degree while teaching. During that time, Texas's state did not allow African Americans to receive graduate degrees, so Prosser obtained her Master's in Education from the University of Colorado, where she also took a multitude of psychology courses. When Prosser graduated, she took a job as a professor, staying there for three years before relocating to Mississippi in 1930. In 1931, Prosser received a grant to conduct doctoral research in teaching and education. Thus, Prosser enrolled at the University of Cincinnati, where she became the first African American woman psychologist in 1933.

Unfortunately, Prosser's life was cut short by a car accident in 1934, a year after receiving her Ph.D. Prosser's contribution to psychology evaluates the racial inequality on African American children's mental health. Prosser conducted her dissertation on "The Non-Academic Development of Negro Children in Mixed and Segregated Schools." Prosser discussed how social factors negatively affect African American children's self-esteem. Prosser's research findings summarized that while segregated schools have comforting aspects, as they are supporting and nurturing; the inequality could have damaging effects such as feelings of isolation and low socioeconomic status. This could have detrimental effects on the child's future and learning opportunities, which become extremely limited by racism.

Prosser's life reminds us of how social barriers prevented African Americans from enjoying the pursuit of happiness regarding the American Dream. The pervasive cycle of struggle as an African American teacher/professor tackles segregation and integrated schools, hoping for an environment for African American children to thrive personally and educationally. As we examine Prosser and her achievements, this book is being written for this same conclusion drawn a century ago. While our schools are no longer segregated, the curriculums are. Unfortunately, our mindsets are on a one-way streak of Whiteness by negating to educate us about Prosser and Black psychology.

*****Inez Beverly Prosser is also considered the first African American woman psychologist. Inez Prosser obtained her doctorate in 1933, and Ruth Howard obtained hers in 1934, but different departments, Education and Psychology, awarded the degrees. Therefore, they were the "firsts" in each department.

Chapter Nine

Kenneth Clark (1940) & Mamie Phipps Clark (1943)
*First African Americans to graduate from Columbia
University with PhDs & Inventors of the Clark Doll
Experiment.*

W hen referring to the Clark's, it is difficult to talk about Kenneth without mentioning Mamie. The Clark's made significant contributions in showing the harmful effects of racial segregation on Black children and conducted extensive research on Race, Self Esteem, and Child Development. During the time period that Kenneth and Mamie were building their foundation in Child Psychology, psychologists taught in colleges such as Erik Erikson and Margaret Mead were also sharing their examinations into children and child-care practices. However, they did not mention the effects of racism on children's racial identity, so Clark's work is truly of great importance.

Kenneth Clark was born in the Panama Canal Zone in 1914, and when his family returned to the United States, they settled in Harlem, New York. After completing high school in New York City, he enrolled in Howard University in Washington D.C. and earned a Bachelor's degree in Psychology in 1935. Howard University is also where he met his future wife, Mamie. After teaching at Howard for one year, he moved back to New York to pursue doctoral studies at Columbia University. Kenneth joined the faculty at The City University of New York, and in 1966, he was the first African American to receive tenure at CUNY. He was also the first African American member of The New York State Board of Regents.

Mamie Phipps was born in Hot Springs, Arkansas, in 1917. By the age of 16, she enrolled at Howard University, obtained her Bachelor's in Psychology, and worked as a secretary in Charles Hamilton Houston's legal office. It was here that Mamie spent her days taking dictation from the pioneers of those who strongly held the desegregation belief, such as Thurgood Marshall, William Hastie, and Charles Houston, and saw the first-hand effects of segregation. She returned to Howard University and obtained her Master's Degree and then earned her Ph.D. from Columbia University. She was the only Black woman in the entire program and the second African American to earn a doctorate at Columbia, with the first being her husband, Kenneth.

In 1946, Mamie and Kenneth founded the Northside Center for Child Development in Harlem, the first agency to offer psychological testing to families living in the area. They were also the creators of "The Clark Doll Test," which was an experiment in which they utilized a Black doll and a white doll to study children's attitudes about race. They asked which doll was nice and which doll was bad, and which doll most looked like the child. The results were that most children identified the Black doll as the bad doll and many children identified themselves with the white doll. The reasoning behind those who identified with the Black doll also disturbed the Clarks, as one boy in Arkansas chose the doll and said, "I'm a nigger. That's a nigger."

This experiment played a substantial role in the Brown vs. the Board of Education case, and Clark's provided expert testimony demonstrating the harmful effects of segregation on children. The Supreme Court ruled that "separate is not equal" and that racial segregation in the United States schools was unconstitutional.

Chapter Ten
Herman George Canady (1941)
First Psychologist to Examine the Role of the Examiner as Bias Factor in IQ Testing

All of Dr. Canady's efforts were solely to create a space for Black psychologists. He was much more than an advocate and ultimately utilized organizations to build up the Black community and increase employment for students who chose to pursue careers in psychology. Herman George Canady was born in 1901 in Oklahoma. In 1927, he received his Bachelor's in Sociology and minored in Psychology. In 1928, he received his Masters in Clinical Psychology, and in 1941, he obtained his Ph.D. in Psychology. All of his degrees were obtained at Northeastern University.

Following Sumner, Canady was the second African American man to obtain a Ph.D. in Psychology as a member within a psychology department, specifically in West Virginia State College. He was the first person to study an examiner's race as a possible source of bias regarding IQ testing and offered suggestions to help mitigate bias and establish a proper environment. His Master's thesis discussed "The Effects of Rapport on the IQ: A Study in Racial Psychology." This thesis was centralized around creating conditions sufficient for testing, in which African American students could thrive. His dissertation, "Test Standing and Social Setting: A Comparative Study of the Intelligence-Test Scores of Negroes Living Under Varied Environmental Conditions," is a widely known and quoted study in psychology and sociology.

Canady also served as a designated diplomat of the American Board of Examiners in Professional Psychology. Canady served as a member on several boards such as the Designated Diplomate of the American Board of Examiners in Professional Psychology, West Virginia Psychological Examiners, and Charleston Guidance Clinic. One of Canady's most important roles was his position as a member of the American Teachers Association, which was a rebuttal response to the National Education Association ban on Black teachers. Through his membership in the ATA, Canady began to organize Black psychologists. Canady created a document named "A Prospectus of an Organization of Negroes Interested in Psychology and Related Fields" and sent the document to ATA members who either worked in psychology or were interested in the cause. He proposed that a psychology section could be formed within the ATA. The department's objective would be "to advance, promote, and encourage the teaching and application of the science of psychology and related fields, particularly in Negro institutions." This department would assist Black institutions with the educational preparation and Black psychologists' hiring. The document also proposed efforts specific to Black institutions to develop an interest in psychology among Black students and enhance research programs pertaining to Black Americans. At the ATA Tuskegee Convention held at the Tuskegee Institute in 1938, Canady presented his ideas to members of the organization. They unanimously voted for forming a Department of Psychology within the ATA. Canady was elected chairman of the group.

Canady spent a lot of his career training and hiring Black psychologists and working closely with NAACP. Canady was utilized for many law cases that ranged from employment discrimination to segregation cases. One of Canady's most controversial but notable publications was *Psychology in Negro Institutions*, which summarized the training and research of Black psychologists in historically Black colleges and universities. This work was controversial because it exposed the current state of psychology education in Black colleges, which was of poor quality due to lack of resources.

Canady's work can be seen through studies that have coined the term "stereotype threat." Stereotype threat is a situational circumstance where people feel themselves at risk of conforming to their social group's stereotype, and the term usually relates to academics. Thus, an example of this would be a white examiner's presence could cause the activation of a stereotype threat in a Black child, where they would expect discrimination, so their IQ test scores would decrease. Evidently, this can be seen in any race. There is a stereotype in which all Asians are considered smart or good in math, and many Asians may feel like they have to be or actually conformed to that stereotype in school. Other studies coined the term "Intergroup anxiety," which is also a result of Canady's work. Intergroup anxiety shows that perceived negative stereotypes can cause the ingroup to become anxious when around the outgroup. An example of this is in the presence of a white examiner; a Black child may perceive the examiner as threatening and untrustworthy, leading to decreased performance on a test.

Chapter Eleven
Margaret Morgan Lawrence (1940)
First African American Woman Psychoanalyst & First Black Female Physician certified by the American Board of Pediatrics.

Margaret Morgan Lawrence was the epitome of if you want something, go get it. Each time she was turned away, she found another opportunity to get her closer to her goal. Lawrence overcame double discrimination of racism and sexism to become the first African American Female Psychiatrist and Psychoanalyst. She retained a noteworthy career in medicine and mental health.

Margaret Morgan Lawrence was born in New York City in 1914 and grew up in Mississippi. She learned that her brother died two years before she was born and dreamed of becoming a doctor to help children just like him. Her brother's death took a toll on her family, and her mother suffered from Depression. Lawrence decided that she would get a better education in New York and moved to live with her aunt in Harlem at the age of 14. After graduating from Cornell University with an outstanding academic record, she was denied acceptance to Cornell's Medical School. With great determination, Lawrence was accepted to The College of Physicians and Surgeons, now Columbia University Vagelos College of Physicians and Surgeons. She was the only

African American graduate of 104 in 1940. She applied to an internship in Babies Hospital but was also rejected because the doctor's residence was only for white men. Instead, Lawrence pursued her career at Harlem Hospital, a training ground that accepted diversity at the time. After the internship ended, she attended Columbia University Mailman School of Public Health in 1943, where she earned her Master of Science. She wanted to learn more about the connection between culture, history, disease, and mental and physical health and worked under Dr. Benjamin Spock's guidance.

During World War II, she taught pediatrics and public health at Meharry Medical College in Nashville, Tennessee. Dr. Lawrence decided to pursue formal training in psychiatry, and in 1948 she became the first African American resident ever admitted to New York Psychiatric Institute; Lawrence enrolled at Columbia University's Columbia Psychoanalytic Center as its first Black trainee and obtained her certification in psychoanalysis. In 1953, Dr. Lawrence moved to Rockland County, New York, where she became the county's first practicing child psychiatrist. Her therapy focused on play and art and integrated Dr. Spock's vision of child, community, and society and explored the connection between physical illness and community health. Lawrence developed some of the first child therapy programs in schools, daycare centers, and hospital clinics.

In 1963, Dr. Lawrence returned to Harlem Hospital to head the Developmental Psychiatry Service, where she worked for more than 20 years. Until 1984, she was an associate clinical professor of psychiatry in the College of Physicians and Surgeons. She served on the New York State Planning Council for Mental Health throughout the 1970s and 1980s. She also wrote two widely used textbooks on treating children with mental impairments named The Mental Health Team in Schools in 1971 and Young Inner-City Families in 1975. In 1998, she received an honorary doctorate of humane letters (L.H.D.) from Berkeley Divinity School at Yale University. In 1992, Dr. Lawrence was awarded the Black Alumni Award by Cornell University. She continued to see patients until she was 90 years old.

Chapter Twelve

Jeanne Spurlock (1947)

First African American Woman to win the Edward A. Strecker, M.D. Award for outstanding contributions to the field of Clinical Psychiatry

Spurlock was born in Sandusky, Ohio, in 1921. Spurlock's journey to medicine came about during the age of nine. During this time, she had a negative experience in the hospital as she was treated for a broken leg and concluded that doctors need to be more caring. Spurlock came from a large family and thought she was too poor to go to medical school, so she initially pursued teaching. After high school, she went to Spelman College in Georgia, but she could not afford to continue, so she relocated to Roosevelt University in Chicago. In 1943, she was accepted into an advanced medical school program at Howard University College, graduating in 1947.

Very few African Americans studied within the field of psychiatry at this time. Spurlock conducted her residency at Chicago's Cook County Hospital in 1950. Her fellowship was done at Juvenile Research in Chicago, and she took a position as a Psychiatrist soon after. In 1953, Spurlock began working toward training as a psychoanalyst at the Chicago Institute for Psychoanalysis and stayed there until 1962, working as a Director of the Children's Psychosomatic Unit at Neuropsychiatric Institute.

From 1960 to 1968, Spurlock was an attending psychiatrist and chief of the Reese Hospital in Chicago. Additionally, she worked as a psychiatrist and chief of the Child Psychiatry Clinic at Michael Reese Hospital in Chicago and an assistant professor of psychiatry at the Illinois College of Medicine, coupled with maintaining her private practice. In 1968, Spurlock was appointed chair of the Department of Psychiatry at Meharry Medicine in Nashville. In 1973, she took a position as a visiting scientist at the National Institute of Mental Health Division of Special Mental Health Programs in Bethesda, Maryland. The following year, Spurlock was awarded Director of American Psychiatric Association's position and held that position through 1991.

Spurlock's work encompassed stressors of poverty, sexism, racism, and discrimination that affect what is known today as the LGBTQ-IA community. She also focused on ambivalent feelings of single Black mothers and absent fathers, which she called "survivor's guilt." Spurlock often lobbied policymakers to ensure funding for medical and post medical education for African Americans could happen. In 1971, she became the first African American and the first woman to win the Edward A. Strecker, M.D. Award for outstanding contributions to clinical psychiatry; in 1988, she was awarded the Solomon Carter Fuller Award to support African Americans' mental health further. In 1994, she won the Alexandra Symonds Association of Women Psychiatrists (AWP) Leadership award. Among her many publications, Spurlock edited *Black*

Psychiatrists and American Psychiatry in 1999. Spurlock paved the way for women in Science, Technology, Engineering, and Math (STEM).

Spurlock's life is impressive between the multitude of awards she won, her capabilities to balance her personal and professional life, her determination and motivation to preserve through poverty up to put herself through school but most importantly, rectifying the misunderstandings in the mental health field through the lens of being an African American woman.

Chapter Thirteen
Maxie Clarence Maultsby Jr. (1957)
Founder of Rational Behavior Therapy

Albert Ellis's name is almost always present when learning about the many therapeutic techniques and orientations. Albert Ellis created Rational-Emotive Therapy, which is considered cognitive behavioral therapy. However, there is no mention of Maxie Clarence Maultsby Jr., who expanded on Ellis's interventions to create Rational Behavior Therapy and found his way working with adults and adolescents. Maultsby was also very aware of the medical field's disparities and mental health for African Americans and expanded on this therapy with that in mind.

Maultsby was born on April 24, 1932, in Pensacola, Florida, to Clarence Maultsby, Sr, and Valdee Campbell Maultsby. The only formal education he received was from his mother for the first seven years of his life. After graduating in 1953 from Talladega College, he received a scholarship to attend Case Western Reserve University in Cleveland, Ohio, to study medicine. In 1957, he received the title, Doctor of Medicine, and in 1962, he served as a military doctor for the United States Air Force. During this time, Maultsby recalled seeing many patients with somatic ailments from unresolved emotional and psychological problems. After four years in the military, he completed a residency in general psychiatry and child and adolescent psychiatry at the University of Wisconsin, where he also taught. He also became a certified sex therapist.

During the time of completing his medical training, Maultsby became great friends with Albert Ellis. He worked very closely with him completing a fellowship in what was then called Rational Emotive Therapy (RET). In 1970, Maultsby created his own Rational Behavior Therapy (RBT), which had similar concepts to RET, but there was a differentiating focus on behavior. Later, Ellis changed his therapy to Rational Emotive Behavior Therapy from Rational-Emotive Therapy and included many behavioral interventions. In 1973, Maultsby established the Training and Treatment Center for Rational Behavior Therapy, and in 1979, he became a professor at the University of Kentucky. He directed the Bryan Psychiatric Hospital in South Carolina and Southern Nevada Adult Mental Health Services. In 1985, Maultsby teamed up with oncologist Dr. O Carl Simonton to combine cognitive behavior therapy with psycho-oncologic interventions, which became a gold standard in psychosocial oncology. In 1989, he was appointed Chairman and Professor of Psychiatry in the College of Medicine at Howard University, where he worked until his retirement in 2004.

Maultsby believed that the distrust African Americans had with mental health professionals was justified and made efforts to make his therapy effective for ethnic minorities, economically disadvantaged, and even illiterate patients. He observed that the short-term efficiency and long-term effectiveness of RBT made it appealing to African Americans and noted that RBT has features that made it culturally conditioned and met African Americans' psychological needs. Maultsby's work is globally recognized and has deeply influenced mental health professionals in the United States, Poland, South Africa, Finland, the Netherlands, and Russia. Many of these books have been translated into many languages, such as Spanish, Swedish, German, Finnish, and Polish. As his therapy is still used today by professionals, RBT is also a self-help tool. He received many awards and honors for his contributions to psychology and psychiatry, including being elected as a Distinguished Life Fellow of the American Psychiatric Association and received a lifetime achievement award from the National Association of Cognitive-Behavior Therapists. He was recognized as one of the 33 African American Medical Pioneers.

Chapter Fourteen
Robert Lee Williams II (1961)
The first Psychologist to Create an IQ test for African Americans and Creator of Terminology (Ebonics)

Williams found a way for African Americans to move forward through Black studies. Born in 1930, an Arkansas native and distinguished university professor, he coined the term 'Ebonics.' There is much to say about his studies and career. Still, it all stems from his time period throughout high school. During his time, aptitude tests were taken to gauge where African Americans were beneficial. Williams' score translated to manual work rather than college, and that took a jab at his confidence for quite some time. Luckily Williams' was surrounded by support and resources, which eventually encouraged and empowered him to make it to college. Williams' graduated from high school, obtained his Bachelor's degree in 1953 and his Masters in 1955. In 1961 Williams earned his Ph.D. in Psychology from Washington University in St. Louis. He co-founded the Department of Black Studies at the University of Washington. Williams went on to teach there from 1970-1992. In 1972, Williams created the "Black Intelligence Test of Cultural Homogeneity " (BITCH-100), which naturally was extremely controversial; as it demonstrated the cultural biases associated with standardized testing. The test had a "combination of dialect and culture-specific verbiage that would enhance the possibility of measuring what is inside the Black child's head. These cultural biases were shown in the same test that Williams took in high school, questioning his self-worth and other detrimental factors. Williams hypothesized that African Americans would do significantly better on the BITCH-100 than conventional tests, and whites would do very poorly. One hundred white and one hundred Black students ranging in ages 16-18, including half from low socioeconomic levels and middle-income levels from the city of St. Louis, took the test. His findings proved that the Black group showed clear superiority over the white group after great data collection and analysis. When given the BITCH-100 and the California Achievement Test to twenty-eight Black "drop out" students from Neighborhood Youth Corps High School, it was clear in regards to the "sensitivity of the BITCH-100 by picking up intellectual indicators that were not commonly found in conventional tests."

The term 'Ebonics' was cultivated from Williams' concept that Ebonics was a psychological language development of African American children. Williams held a national conference in 1973 in St. Louis, and the conception was born. In 1975 Williams' published a book, *Ebonics: The True Language of Black Folks*. This literature has an in-depth approach to defining the terminology Ebonics and discussing how slang is a flawed form of Eurocentric English culture.

Chapter Fifteen
Joseph L. White (1961)
Founder of Educational Opportunities Program at
California State University and Cofounder of the
Association of Black Psychologists

Coined the "Godfather of Black psychology" (Sumner is the "father"), Joseph White helped steer the conversation of inclusivity in regard to mental health for African Americans. He knew and understood that the African American experience contrasted with the white American experience, which needed to be addressed in psychology. He ultimately helped create a network of profound, ethnically diverse psychologists through his platform where Black presence was scarce.

Joseph White was born on December 19, 1932, in Nebraska but grew up in Minnesota. When his mother became worried that White was associating with the wrong crowd, she made him live with his sister in San Francisco, California. When White realized he could not obtain a job waiting tables at nicer restaurants in San Francisco due to discriminatory laws, his sister convinced him to attend college. He received a Bachelor's Degree at San Francisco State University, served two years in the United States Army, and then enrolled in a Masters Program at San Francisco State University. In 1958, he enrolled in the clinical psychology Ph.D. program at Michigan State

University and, in 1961, became the first Black doctoral graduate at that college.

White moved back to California to teach at California State University in Long Beach with his doctorate. Despite having a high paying job, White still could not buy a home in the neighborhood he wanted and began to realize that these discriminatory practices were not only happening to him but it was systemic. In 1967, he created the Educational Opportunities Program (EOP) at the Long Beach campus, which eventually led to the program's system-wide development. This program provided educational access to more than 250,000 low income and educationally disadvantaged students throughout California. EOP can now be noticed in many colleges across the nation, directly influenced by White. In 1968, Dr. White worked with representatives in the state legislature, like Willie Brown, to bring about the passage of the Harmer Bill SB 1072, the bill that established the funding for EOP Programs in California. He returned to San Francisco State College and became a professor of psychology and dean of undergraduate studies. In 1968, he helped establish the first Black studies program at the college and worked tirelessly to make education accessible to all.

After the displeasing meeting with APA leadership, White helped found the Association of Black Psychologists. In 1970, White wrote an article in *Ebony* magazine, *Toward a Black Psychology*, which brought a greater understanding of the differences in how African Americans should be treated and understood in psychology. That article is credited as the spark that helped build upon Black psychology today. The next year, he began teaching at UC Irvine. For the rest of his career, he would remain there as supervising psychologist and director of ethnic studies and cross-cultural programs, mentoring over 100 students. While at Irvine, White wrote several books, including 1984's *The Psychology of Blacks: An African-American Perspective,* 1989's *The Troubled Adolescent,* and 1999's *Black Man Emerging.* He also served on the California State Psychology Licensing Board, chairing it for three years.

White was the recipient of many prestigious awards, including the Citation of Achievement in Psychology and Community Service from President Clinton in 1994, the honorary Doctor of Laws from the University of Minnesota in 2007, and Alumnus of the Year from San Francisco State University in 2008. He also received a presidential citation from the American Psychological Association to honor his career achievements.

Chapter Sixteen
Kobi Kambon AKA. Joseph A. Baldwin (1975)
Creator of African American Centered World Views and
Philosophies

Kobi Kambon, aka. Joseph A. Baldwin dedicated his life's work to African-centered or Black psychology. His psychological stance was profound as he chose to spotlight African American psychology and differentiated it from white psychology. Quite frankly, he challenged Eurocentric studies related to African Americans and empowered African Americans to embrace their roots and culture. As an educator and psychologist, he focused heavily on African Americans' mental health, cultural oppression and created tools for professionals in the mental health field to understand the Black experience.

Dr. Kambon was born on November 29, 1943, in Alabama to Mable E. Guyton-Baldwin and Andrew Baldwin Sr. Kambon. He was the ninth of ten children, with four sisters and five brothers. In 1969, he obtained his Bachelor's degree in Psychology from DePaul University in Chicago and then acquired his Master's in Personality Abnormal Psychology in 1971 from Roosevelt University. Finally, he received his Ph.D. in Personality and Social Psychology from the University of Colorado in 1975.

Dr. Kambon retired from working as a psychology professor at the Psychology Department at Florida A&M University. He held the department chair from 1985-1997 and served as the community graduate program coordinator. During his 30 year career, he emphasized Afrocentric views, which helped shape the Department of Psychology and increased the number of psychology graduates of African descent. As a result, Florida A&M psychology's department became one of the country's highest producing departments.

In his article *African (Black) Psychology: Issues and Synthesis,* Dr. Kambon provided an overview of his approach to studying Black Americans' psychology and suggested that it is entirely separate from Western psychology. He thought that those who study Black psychology that is "contained" within Western psychology are stuck within a Eurocentric psychology framework. He insisted that conceptualizing Black psychology independently of Western psychology is reasonable because African cultures existed and preceded Western cultures. He advocated for a Black psychology that allowed African Americans to resist European reality structures in favor of an African worldview that affirmed their existence and restored what Kambon called "Africanity."

Dr. Kambon saw African Americans' mental health concerns as distortions of the African personality from its natural condition. He coined the terms "African self-extension orientation" and "African self-consciousness." African self-extension orientation refers to the African American personalities that are innately different from European personalities. African self-consciousness is the expression of self that is constantly regulated by environmental context, so the full expression of African personalities is based on the alignment of oneself related to culture or "African cosmology." He proposed interventions to restore African Self Consciousness with African self-extension orientation by reinforcing institutional structures that supported African cultures, such as Afrocentric educational institutions, religious institutions, social activities, and rituals.

He created tools such as the African Self-Consciousness Scale (ASCS), The Worldviews Scale (WVS), and The Cultural Misorientation Scale (CMS), which measured personality, mental health, and social variables that captured the Black experience. He has more than 60 scholarly publications, including five books, two widely used among professionals and students in psychology and Black studies departments. These books' names are African/ Black psychology in the American Context (1988) and The African Personality in America (1992). He is also the former National President of The Association of Black Psychologists (ABPsi). Dr. Kambon was awarded Board Certification as a Diplomat and Fellow in African-Centered/ Black psychology.

Chapter Seventeen
The Association of Black Psychologists (ABPsi)

Black Psychologists created the Association of Black Psychologists (ABPsi) in San Francisco in 1968. This organization was cultivated to address Black psychologists' many problems as professionals. The objective is to support the Black community by developing ways to support Blacks affected by social problems and influence change to accommodate their needs. This once small-scale organization has now grown to over 1400 members. With about 106 thousand psychologists in America and Black psychologists making up about 4 percent of that population, the organization should be composed of at least 4k Black psychologists. We need to network and support organizations as such to build our empire.

Membership Benefits

- Free subscription to *The Journal of Black Psychology* annually
- Free subscription to *The Psych Discourse News Journal* annually
- Free access to ABPsi's on-line Career Center
- Exclusive member opportunity to submit articles for consideration of publication in ABPsi journals
- Exclusive member inclusion in ABPsi's Psychologist Resource Directory via the ABPsi website

- Reduced Annual Convention registration fees
- Voting privileges (except for Affiliate members)
- Mentoring opportunities
- Intellectual stimulation
- Participation in an organization committed to the physical, mental, and spiritual well-being of African people

Chapter Eighteen
Black Psychiatrists of America (BPA)

Black Psychiatrists of America has been "Lifting minds since 1969." This organization was created by Black psychiatrists, who understood that support and resources were needed for Black psychiatrists, as they persistently dealt with racism. This organization provides Black psychiatrists with a Black community that acts as a safe space. This organization has largely contributed to the success of Black psychiatry. Black psychiatrists have always struggled with social conditions as society has never prioritized African American mental health needs. This "action-oriented" organization addresses the many brown faces of Black psychiatry that have been wronged and provide corrective actions in the fight for equality.

Membership Benefits

- Membership Discounts on Conferences & Continuing Medical Education
- Membership Discounts on Supplies, Services, and Branded Products
- BPA Journal
- Voting Representation
- Physician Locator Service
- Public Relations

"The Black Psychiatrists of America have a heterogeneous membership woven of every culture of African descent. Our communities are bound by a common thread but fractured by structural racism, colonialism, and autochthonous identities. The BPA appreciates these differences with an intent to dissolve any barriers that separate us. Every person has a right to a free mind, freedom from the mental stress of racism and mental illness, but when present a right to health care. Psychiatry is political. When once nations exiled dissidents, the system now weaponizes psychological diagnoses and treatments. Those who may not be mentally ill are made sick to serve structural racism and mass incarceration. It subjects children and adults to psychological tests that have not been validated or published in referred journals, so mental health practitioners act as magistrates to support mass incarceration. As a matter of justice, the BPA pathway forward moves from consumers to producers of knowledge. What we reformulate must be well defined, withstand refutation, and applicable to survival in everyday life."

- Dr. Benjamin Roy March 2021
    Current President of Black Psychiatrists of America

Chapter Nineteen

Assessment: The Journey to Culturally Sensitive Psychological Testing

ssessments are utilized a great deal in mental health counseling. It is usually used to diagnose psychological disorders, verify health insurance coverage, create mental health groups and workshops, and assess personality traits and advisement for legal matters. It was thought that many of these assessments were objective and generalizable to all ethnic groups, even though results showed that assessments were standardized, valid, and reliable with primarily white, middle-class English language samples. As we begin to understand the biases that many psychological and educational assessments have today, it should be known that assessments were biased against people of color from its conception.

The foundation of modern standardized testing has its roots in the Eugenics Movement that lasted from the late 1800s to the early 1900s. Francis Galton coined the term Eugenics which meant "good stock" and meant that certain racial groups were superior to others. At the time, this influenced the thought that certain behaviors could be reasoned based on genetics. Galton's cousin, Charles Darwin, wrote a book on a natural selection called *On the Origin of Species* in 1859, which explained the idea that certain species would advance while others would die off. In 1864, Herbert Spencer advanced the "survival of the fittest" ideas. He wrote *Principles of Biology*, advocating for segregated societies with birth control, restrictive marriages, and the sterilization of people who were considered inferior. From 1907 to 1930, 30 states in the United States enacted sterilization laws for "inferior people." Intelligent Quotient or IQ tests, such as the Stanford Binet Intelligence Test was used to identify individuals who were thought to be inferior. California had by far the highest number of sterilizations in the United States, which accounted for one-third of all sterilizations nationwide. Of the total sterilizations, almost 60% were considered mentally ill, and more than 35% were considered mentally deficient. Men and women of Mexican origin represented between 7% and 8% of those sterilized (Stern, *Eugenic Nation*, p. 111). African Americans made up 1% of California's population but accounted for 4% of the sterilizations (Stern, *Eugenic Nation*, p. 111).

The Stanford Binet Intelligence test was created by Albert Binet, Victor Henri, and Theophile Simon under Lewis Terman's leadership in 1916. Binet and Simon used the mental measurement classifying individuals as idiots, imbeciles, and morons. Terman would later revise these measurements, using words such as "borderline deficiency" and upholding that this deficiency is common in Mexicans and Blacks. This "dullness" seems to be a racial matter. In 1917, Clarence Yoakum and Robert Yerkes created the Army Alpha and Army Beta tests to classify people of different backgrounds to determine who should serve in World War I as office men or infantrymen. The Alpha test was for those who were literate, and the Beta test was for those who were illiterate, and ultimately, it was a biased test to determine who would be in the front lines fighting. Those that were non-European scored low, which made them fit for the infantry position and not an officer. The Army's Alpha and Beta tests formed the basis for the Verbal (Alpha) and Nonverbal (Beta) test concepts that have long characterized modern-day IQ tests. Wechsler's nonverbal tests were taken directly from the Army Beta tests, and while some have been removed from the core Wechsler scale, others are still used.

In early 1950, racial segregation within the United States school system was normal. Following the Brown vs. Board of Education (1954), "separate educational facilities are inherently unequal" doctrine, intelligence testing was often used to place students of color into general education classes designated for "slow learners" or special education classes. This tracking of students of color created schools built by "de facto" segregation. In 1969, the Association of Black Psychologists published this policy statement:

The Association of Black Psychologists fully supports those parents who have chosen to defend their rights by refusing to allow their children and themselves to be subjected to achievement, intelligence, aptitude, and performance tests, which have been and are being used to (a) label Black people as uneducable; (b) place Black children in "special" classes and schools; (c) potentiate inferior education; (d) assign Black children to lower educational tracks than whites; (e) deny Black students higher educational opportunities; and (f) destroy positive intellectual growth and development of Black children. (Williams et al., 1980 p. 265–266)

It became apparent that intelligence tests were being used to place students of color into special education, which can still be seen today as Black children are underrepresented in gifted and talented programs. According to the U.S. Department of Education's Office of Civil Rights (2012), Black students' placement in special education has increased every year since 1968; Black students are overrepresented in the categories of intellectual disability and emotional disturbance (Hosp & Reschly, 2004). Black students in special education are more likely to have more restrictive placements, such as self-contained classrooms, compared to students of other ethnicities. They spend more time away from the general education population than white students. Many educational facilities remain segregated due to socioeconomic status within society. This form of modern segregation is far from a myth and very damaging to low-income African Americans. Much like systemic racism, matriculated Whiteness came about because no stipulation outlined how Americans would implement integration moving forward. This has caused a harmful loophole that has psychologically imprisoned African Americans' minds for far too long and must be dismantled. Traditional intelligence testing does not measure intelligence if there is a known equity gap in predominantly Black schools versus predominately white schools. Not to be confused in inequality, inequity does mean unfairness but is seen on the individual level. In the school system, equity asks what individual students need to succeed? In underfunded schools, that question cannot be asked because there isn't funding to execute resources needed for individual students. Poor school instruction, fewer academic resources coincided with the fundamental thought that you may be inferior to another, will skew an intelligence testing result. There is no question that vocabulary words and mathematical equations are necessary to determine if a child may need extra services but should not put any child at a disadvantage.

Neighborhood wealth plays a crucial part in education but especially regarding minorities. It is a known fact that many low-income African American schools are under-resourced, outdated, and students, due to many environmental factors, may engage in school violence. Additionally, a lot of those issues are never addressed. High poverty African American saturated schools are falling apart, and most need to be updated and have their systems revamped desperately. Ignored infrastructure problems lead to many medical issues and result in student absenteeism, negatively affecting students' academic performance. Thus, low-poverty districts do not have local revenue to fund reconstruction for the number of repairs needed, coupled with yearly massive education budget cuts; the pervasive cycle continues.

We are all cultural beings that hold biases, some that we are aware of, and others not so much. There is no clear cut path to reducing biases in assessment, but one way to do so is to become more aware of what is being administered to specific clients. Those in the mental health field need to become more aware of certain assessments' purpose and the potential biases the assessments may have. These professionals must also know African Americans' history, how the test is administered, and learn about the interpretation and conclusions deduced when working with people of color. It is known that many of these assessments have been standardized based on the Eurocentric population, so we must begin to find culturally sensitive assessments.

For African Americans who are seeking mental health care, there will be certain assessments that must be administered. Do not be afraid to ask questions and research more about the assessments you are given. A plethora of assessments can be administered for certain diagnoses, and the DSM-5 includes a great deal of culturally sensitive and relevant assessments that should be provided to you. When the assessment results are given, if you do not feel like it captures your symptoms or experiences, let the professional know. Counseling requires that clients are active participants in their treatment, and although you may not be aware of the interactives of assessments, you may ask questions related to your therapy. After reading about the history of assessments, it is detrimental to your wellbeing that these topics are discussed more in mental health settings.

Chapter Twenty

Modern 21st Century "Black Intelligence Test of Cultural Homogeneity" (BITCH-100)[1]

There is great difficulty finding Robert Lee William's original complete BITCH-100 test. Therefore, we decided to create our own version of his test to give readers a complete example based on current times named the Modern 21st Century "Black Intelligence Test of Cultural Homogeneity" (BITCH-100).

However, we also wanted to include and reference two examples on William's test. Some of the examples on his test included:

1. Clean
   A. just out of the bathtub
   B. very well dressed
   C. Indian
   D. had a great deal

2. Blood
   A. a vampire
   B. a dependent individual
   C. an injured person

---

[1] "Black Intelligence Test of Cultural Homogeneity" (BITCH-100) Example

D. a brother of color

Modern 21st Century "Black Intelligence Test of Cultural Homogeneity" (BITCH-100).

1. "Bread" means
   A. Dough
   B. Money
   C. Biscuit
   D. Muffin

2. "That's wild" means
   A. Animal-like
   B. Non-domestic
   C. Crazy
   D. Barbaric

3. "IKYFL" means
   A. I Know You F*cn Lyin'!
   B. I Know You Farted Loud!
   C. I Know You Fell Left!
   D. I Know You Fainted Late!

4. "TBH" means
   A. To Be Honest
   B. Tomato Bacon Ham
   C. The branch hangs
   D. That boy hangry

5. "Lit" means
   A. Fire
   B. Fun
   C. Illuminating
   D. Burning

6. "I'm weak " means
   A. Fragile
   B. Delicate
   C. Sick
   D. Really Funny

7. "Netflix and Chill" means
   A. Watch TV + Sex
   B. Subscription
   C. Relax
   D. Stay Home

8. "Bae" means
   A. Pet
   B. Parents
   C. Sibling
   D. Significant Other

9. "The Itis" means
   A. Disease
   B. Sleepy and Full
   C. Disorder
   D. Nickname

10. "Snatched" means
    A. Kidnapped
    B. Taken Abruptly
    C. Without Permission
    D. Looks Really Good, On Point

11. "Lowkey" means
    A. Attention
    B. Making Noise
    C. Secretly
    D. Obvious

12. "No Cap" means
    A. Without a Hat
    B. Scalp Exposed
    C. Lost Head Attire
    D. No lie, For Real

13. "Flex" means
    A. Show Muscles
    B. Body Builder
    C. Reflexes
    D. To Show Off

14. "Slayed" means
    A. Slaughter
    B. Strongly Impress
    C. Violence
    D. Kill

15. "Curve" means
    A. To take a turn
    B. To reject someone
    C. To throw a curveball
    D. To deviate from a straight line

16. "Sus" means
    A. Suggestive
    B. Successful
    C. Suing
    D. Suspicious

17. "Tea" means
    A. Gossip
    B. Beverage
    C. Plant
    D. Drink

18. "Extra" means
    A. Additional
    B. Excessive, dramatic behavior
    C. Exceptional
    D. Supplement

19. "Salty" means
    A. Mineral composed of sodium chloride
    B. Seasoning
    C. Upset or bitter as a result of embarrassment
    D. Grainy

20. "Issa Mood" means
    A. Upsetness
    B. Bi-Polar Disorder
    C. Conscious state of mind
    D. Vibe

21. "Karen" mean
    A. Female
    B. Oblivious Racist White Women
    C. Name of a person
    D. Male

22. "Slaps" means
    A. To Hit
    B. To Be Excellent or Amazing
    C. To Fight
    D. To Slam

23. "Shade" means
    A. Darkness
    B. A Color
    C. Shelter
    D. Rude or Slick Comment

24. "Basic" means
    A. Fundamental
    B. Ordinary
    C. Essential
    D. Essence

25. "Cancelled" means
    A. Rid Of
    B. Discontinued Support
    C. Delete
    D. Discard

26. "Fire" means
    A. Burning Passion
    B. Inspiration
    C. Cool/Great
    D. Chemical Process

27. "Deadass" means
    A. Death
    B. Are You Serious?
    C. Anus
    D. To Push

28. "Big Mad" means
    A. Mentally ill
    B. Extremely Upset
    C. Remarkable
    D. Enthused

29. "Drip" means
    A. Drooling
    B. Spilled Liquid
    C. Leaking
    D. Cool/Sexy Sense of Style

30. " SMH" means
    A. Shaking My Head
    B. Sugar Milk Hot Chocolate
    C. So Much Honey
    D. Sheep May Hop

Chapter Twenty-One
Black History is American History: Promoting Blackness

During The Great Migration, more than six million African Americans relocated from the South to the Northern states due to dissatisfactory economic opportunities and harsh segregationist laws. From 1916 to 1970, many African Americans attempted to take advantage of industrial workers' needs that arose from World War I. After the Civil War and during the Reconstruction era, segregationist laws such as Jim Crow became the law of the land in the South. Even though the Ku Klux Klan was abolished in 1869, they continued underground and engaged in violence, harassment, and intimidation, including the lynching of African Americans.

While African Americans were emancipated and the Northern states promised a better life, racism and prejudice continued. Northern racism was groomed and grew from the customs cultivated from slavery and thought processes that justified involuntary Whiteness. The very concept of Blacks and Whites was planted on American soil. The "Age of the Common Man' manifested new meanings that were never before possessed, solely to benefit Whites only, specifically white men. No matter how poor white people were, they considered themselves superior to Blacks simply by being white.

In response to this prejudice, African Americans did not simply sit back and accept it. Since residential neighborhoods made agreements not to sell housing to Black people, many ended up creating their own cities within big cities, which helped stimulate a new urban, African American culture. A distinguished example of this was Harlem in New York City, an all-white neighborhood that, by the 1920s, housed some 200,000 African Americans. During the Great Migration, the Black experience became an important theme in the artistic movement known first as the New Negro Movement and later as the Harlem Renaissance. The Great Migration also began a new era of increasing political activism among African Americans, who, after being disenfranchised in the South, found a new place for themselves in public life in the Northern and Western cities. There were known conventions to discuss legal measures and corrective courses of action that protected fugitives and saved free Blacks from being rekidnapped and re-sold to the South. African Americans founded their own businesses, from churches to schools. The formation of Black Wall Street in Tulsa, Oklahoma, was strictly created to provide resources, support, empower and encourage the African American community to excel and promote Blackness. It became known as the most prosperous African American community in the United States. However, on May 31st of 1921, racial violence destroyed thirty-five city blocks with fire that caused the death of 36 people. Still, historians have estimated the death toll to be about 300. Residents and businesses were attacked, and it remains one of the worst incidents of racial violence in the United States. As Black Wall Street threatened white America's capitalism, this was a response, shown in violence.

The intentional deletion of African American history should fuel us to unfold our blackness's hidden layers. African Americans must commit to educating ourselves and others within our community. We need to always intentionally seek out resources to learn about our historical backdrop as African Americans in America. We should be intentional and consistent about changing systemic racism; combating the many raw forms of inequality requires the African American community to join together as one. We need to make the lack of adequate mental health, medical, and injustices with the law a top priority. The inequitable access to advanced and rigorous coursework, unsafe and unhealthy school environments, and Eurocentric education systems disproportionately harm African Americans' overall well-being. Change needs to be demanded from local school board meetings up through state capitols. Given the sacrifices made by former African American women and men psychologists and psychiatrists, particular emphasis should be placed on educational institutions related to the curriculum/syllabus to highlight the importance of representation in Black communities. Many of the curriculums taught in the classrooms can be rewritten to tell African Americans' history, as there are actual entities and literature that focus on these changes. School-aged children should also be provided textbooks that inform them of people who have contributed to a society that look like them. Ultimately, the changes should reflect diversity and inclusion.

In 1787, the three-fifths compromise amendment verbalized that each enslaved African American counted as three/fifths of a person. It's hard not to correlate that very distasteful and disturbing notion to the fact that historically, the census has disproportionately undercounted the African American population for decades. This directly affects systemic racism because there are missing data results and missing dollars and funds that could have been allocated based on Census Bureau Data. Thus, Federal dollars concerning Black communities are lost alongside African Americans' miscount. If the allocation of funds has a great deal to do with dividing money per population, but African Americans are being undercounted, how do we not expect systemic racism to be at the forefront of underfunding throughout Black communities? This complex formula is disastrous and directly affects Black educational institutions. It would benefit African Americans to advocate for the community to ensure that the necessary tax funds are allocated to the proper entities so that there are no restrictions based on where they live. There need to be more conversations that discuss the importance of prioritizing filling out the census and making sure it is filled out correctly and on time.

For African Americans who work in majority-white environments, assimilating to the dominant culture may have been a way to survive, but it may actually be detrimental to one's identity. Being able to express yourself, wear your hair the way you want it, whether it is an afro or dreadlocks is a form of Black expression and culture. Having to assimilate to the white dominant culture takes away an important aspect of an African American's being. Changing a hairstyle or talking a certain way translates to the non-acceptance of your authentic selves. If one can figure out the types of persons in the workplace that can assist in and have a conversation about promoting inclusion and diversity, it is beneficial to overall well-being and promotes Blackness.

Supporting Black-owned businesses is not a task or trend; it is a lifestyle. Take ownership in choosing to be why the Black community has opportunities, property ownership, credit building, and generational wealth. Most importantly, supporting African Americans is celebrating Black culture with visibility and representation. As Issa Rae said, "'I'm rooting for anyone who's Black," and that stands at the core of the mentality needed to promote Blackness continuously.

Chapter Twenty-Two
Black Burnout: Self Care

Think about what mental health means to you and how you plan to sustain and strengthen your state of well-being.

If you are Black, another layer is added that questions how do you do all of that while being Black in America? Recently, the words ``self-care'' has been used heavily to put emphasis on what everyone should be doing to keep themselves physically, mentally and emotionally healthy. While this is true for everyone, African Americans should unquestionably and undoubtedly practice self-care due to the injustices of racism that are experienced each day. Many of us have been traumatized and many others have been desensitized to the murders of Black people by the hands of police officers. Subtly, in relation to the healthcare field, there are racial disparities as African Americans are less likely to receive preventive health services but are likely to receive lower-quality care. The reasons continue as Black people face discrimination, prejudice, microaggressions and inequality in their everyday life but are expected to be productive and level-headed human beings. There is no assistance or "safe haven" put in place to help African Americans unwind or feel safe in America, so mental health must be a priority every time.

Oftentimes, there is the perception that self care has to be an extravagant activity that costs a great deal of money, such as getting a massage or taking an expensive trip. While those activities are also considered self care, in general self care does not have to cost money at all. Self care can be defined as any activity that protects the emotional, psychological and social well-being of a person, whether that is taking a long bath to cooking a favorite meal or spending time with a loved one. One great venture that emphasizes the essence of wellness is partaking in mindful practices. The essence of mindfulness is rooted in meditation, which consists of slow breathing and clearing the mind. These practices aid to ease the mind and helps the person become more present and self aware. Whenever you are able to, take some time to put the phone down and breathe, noticing the sensations in your body. That is the time to check in with yourself and listen to what your body may be telling you. Do you need extra sleep or is there a pain that you've been ignoring all day and now you can finally tend to it? Throughout the day, it is hard to do these check in's, depending on how hectic the day may be, so it is essential to give yourself these moments at some point during the day. Some activities that are considered mindful are adult coloring books or "Paint and Sip," in which you are drinking a glass of the liquor of your choice while painting your very own masterpiece.

When protests relating to racial injustice occur, it is important that you know what part you want to partake in. If you are joining the protests, that is significant. If you decide that you want to live vicariously through those who advocate and protest, that is also significant.

There is no "right" way to show your support and to advocate for others, but do not feel that you are not doing enough. You can support based on your comfortability and what promotes the cause based on your principles or morals, while being fair to yourself. Sometimes, when on social media it is easy to fall into the trap of comparing yourself to others and the impact they may be making. What you are not seeing is their self care practices at the end of the day to engage in this type of work. If you are the one actively protesting and finding outlets to speak try to help those who are still finding their voice. Follow positive Black leaders on social media that speak to who you are and advocate for causes dear to you because they will also be able to provide you with ways you can advocate and assist that may be aligned with your advocacy archetype.

Combat isolation through connection. Learn who you can speak to about your racial injustices for purposes of recharging. Unearth who you can unpack with to receive all of you, especially when you are vulnerable. This is detrimental to your well being. We are bombarded with news everyday whether it is on television or social media, but the injustices are seen and must be processed with others. We are social beings and thrive through understanding, so when we are able to relate to others it can perpetuate feelings of safety, creating a harmonious relationship. Usually, African Americans are able to easily connect with other African Americans, based on shared experiences and there is nothing faulty with that. Similarly to finding the right Black therapist, having a Black friend is just as important and undeniably gives the same benefits. At the finish line, connection will award you with your personal community.

Chapter Twenty-Three

*What do you look for when choosing a therapist as an
African American?*

***The word "therapist" is used in this chapter but
does encompass different providers in the field
such as Psychologist, Psychiatrist, Mental Health
Counselor, and Social Worker***

Let's suppose that you are an African American male or female going through a lot in life or know that some possible childhood trauma may be showing itself in certain relationships. Maybe you just need someone to talk to or may be suffering from a mental disorder that you knowingly have been trying to suppress for a long time but can no longer. You decide that you would like to seek out a therapist. You go online and complete a quick google search, typing "therapists near me." This search results in a plethora of sites naming *Psychology Today, Zocdoc*, and *Better Help* as the top links. With a quick click on *Zocdoc*, an instant list of therapists is shown, and as you scroll, you see no one that looks like you. There is a running list of 100+ pages of white therapists. You feel defeated, and with a tinge of annoyance, you put your phone away and continue with your day promising yourself that you will do another search tomorrow.

This is the reality of being African American and searching for the "right" therapist. This does not mean that an African American cannot see a white therapist and build a bond. However, the issue lies in the statistics presented earlier in the book, 4% of the psychologists in America are Black. When a person of color decides that they want to see a therapist after fighting through cultural deterrents or deep-rooted stigmas of mental health and do not see anyone who looks like them, their search journey comes to a standstill. Life continues, and that person will continue to fight through whatever is bothering them. This problem is a recurring theme; representation matters. African Americans may feel more comfortable and may feel like their therapist actually understands what they are going through as Black men or women living in America when they have a therapist that looks like them. Through Robert Lee William's BITCH-100, and the 21st century one that we created, it is evident that Black people have their own vernacular, which is how they understand and relate to each other, especially when comfortable. With that being said, the way that the problem may be explained through this vernacular requires multicultural counseling. Many African American therapists recognize and acknowledge this when in therapy. There are many things that an African American could look for when seeking a therapist. Aside from not finding therapists that look like you, looking through a running list of hundreds of therapists can be overwhelming. It is necessary to recognize what is important when reading about a therapist and how to find possible matches.

Usually, during the first session, a therapist will give a client a document called informed consent. Informed consent is information that a client must read through thoroughly, as it contains information about the therapist, their fees, theoretical orientation, therapy process, and legal information. Some therapists may include a minuscule version of this in their biography on the site sponsoring them or on their personal website. It is always a good sign when a therapist provides information on what to expect in therapy. If that information is provided, read through it thoroughly as it is a good indication of what you can expect, and you can make a better judgment of whether or not you would like to work with them. This tactic can also narrow down the list instead of scrolling through therapists who only provide one line of what they specialize in or do not include a biography. If a therapist catches your eye that does not have a biography or explain their therapy process, here are some questions you may want to ask:

- What is your theoretical orientation, or how do you conceptualize problems?
- How much experience do you have with (___insert problem/issue/disorder here?___)
- What are your thoughts on, or do you have any multicultural counseling experience?
- In general, how do you run your individual counseling sessions?

The next piece of information to look for on a therapist's page is specializations. Usually, therapists do not specialize in every disorder or problem, so it is important to look for this information to see if that specific counselor can help you on your therapeutic journey. Some may specialize in Post Traumatic Stress Disorder and Anxiety when others may specialize in life transitions and completing life goals. You may have an idea of what you need assistance within your life, so follow your gut feeling and pick a therapist based on what you think you may need.

Looking at the therapists' fees is also helpful, as only you know how much you can afford. Some therapists may take insurance, so narrowing down your search based on your personal insurance can be useful. However, the therapist list that takes your insurance may be minimal. Many therapists may have a sliding scale, which means that the price is based on the client's ability to pay. The fee may be reduced for clients with lower incomes or those who may have less money to spare after their personal expenses are paid. During the first session, the client and therapist will have an opportunity to talk about the fee, and you must be honest about how much you are willing to pay.

The therapist's picture is important, but do not decide on a therapist solely based on how he/she looks. The therapist's age is information that you may use at your discretion. Some may want an older therapist, as they may feel like they have more years and experience in the field. Some may want a younger therapist, someone who possibly has a better handle on current times. Implicit biases come into play here, and being aware of that will assist you on this journey. Determine the prospective age you may want your therapist to be and why. Asking yourself these questions will help you gain a greater understanding of who you are and the type of people you may be vulnerable with. During therapy, plenty of emotions will surface, some positive and negative. It is important that you feel comfortable enough to talk about the negative ones with your therapist and formulate a plan to work through them. Therapy is not one-sided, so it is of great significance that you are present from the beginning. Therefore, being present in the "searching" stage is just as valuable.

Be sure to self reflect after each therapy session. Since you have been going to therapy, have you seen change or progress based on the goals set in therapy? Do you feel like you are becoming a better version of yourself? Are you able to process any significant events and emotions that derived during those events? Are you able to use what is taught in therapy in your everyday life? Do you feel understood and able to share your true self with the therapist, without feelings of judgement? The answers to these questions are vital even when you have found a Black therapist.

"This therapist made me feel worse but I look at her and see myself."

It may feel catastrophic and overwhelming if you do find a Black therapist that makes your therapeutic experience disastrous, where you actually feel worse after talking to the person. This isn't exclusive at all to Black therapists, but the main focus is on Black therapists in this chapter. Therefore, if you do happen to have this experience, be sure that you can terminate therapy with that person and find another. The experience may dampen your spirits, but that is why this chapter is dedicated to helping find a therapist for you, as an African American. That person's therapeutic style did not mesh with your being, and sometimes that happens. Do not internalize these feelings with thoughts that you cannot get "better" or that no one can "fix" you based on these experiences. You do not need to be fixed or to be normal, you just need to be yourself. One tip is to treat finding the "right" therapist as dating. Sometimes the therapist you thought was the one was in fact not the one for you and that is okay.

Black Therapist Websites

Black Female Therapists: blackfemaletherapists.com
Black Therapists Rock: blacktherapistsrock.com
Therapy For Black Girls: therapyforblackgirls.com
Therapy for Black Men: therapyforblackmen.org
Melanin and Mental Health:
melaninandmentalhealth.com
Clinicians of Color: clinicansofcolor.org
Root to Crown Healing: roottocrownhealing.com

Black Mental Health Organizations

Black Emotional and Mental Health (BEAM)
Black Mamas Matter Alliance (BMMA)
Black Mental Health Alliance (BMHA)
Black Mental Health Wellness (BMHW)
Black Women's Health Imperative (BWHI)
Inclusive Therapists

LGBTQ Psychotherapists of Color
Melanin and Mental Health
National Association of Black Counselors (NABC)
National Association of Black Social Workers (NABSW)
National Queer and Trans Therapists of Color Network
The Okra Project

Summary

Being a well known white psychologist because of involuntary educational Whiteness through Eurocentric curriculums does not equate to being a top Psychologist; it is simply a poor attempt to interrupt Blackness. Microinvalidations have gone on far too long in America. Ironically, African American psychologists are routinely excluded, negated, or nullified as influential. All of which is entirely incorrect; we must continue to unmask racial microaggressions. Racism is not as subtle as we are led to believe, and much of what occurs is intentional. This book is packed with Black established psychologists whose research and contribution to psychology speak for themselves. Organizations such as American Psychological Association (APA) produced an article in 2002 called "*Eminent Psychologists of the 20th Century,* " including 99 Psychologists, none of which are from this book. Most importantly, none are African American. Daily racial socialization regarding academics has unfavorable psychological outcomes, and the perception of lack of representation attributes to mental health disparities among African Americans. Our sense of belongingness and overall well-being as African Americans become challenged when acculturation is predominantly white.

Our book concludes that we ultimately do better when we know better, but resources need to be readily available to make that actual statement realistic. This journey began with having no clear understanding of who paved the way for our successes as African American mental health providers. After much has been addressed and acknowledged, one can appreciate our journey as African Americans in the United States. It's admirable that despite the continual up current of events within the United States, which range from slavery, injustice, systemic racism, discrimination, police brutality, we continue to defy societal normalities and push through making way for ourselves. We continue to show that we, in fact, belong here, and we will be seen as law-abiding citizens who made their mark in this country despite not always being accepted.

Nicól and Tamera have chosen to take on this moral obligation to pay our respects to African American psychologists/psychiatrists who have been disregarded as high ranking amongst what we consider momentous clinicians. This book is detailed and highlighted, reiterating how scientific racism contributes to the perception that African Americans are inferior when indeed, we are equal and, in some cases, superior within itself due to how diverse data collection amongst other factors are resulting in inaccurate research findings. European scientists could never articulate our Blackness through their white only literature and lens of how they view their world. There is nothing more gratifying than being authors who are addressing disproportionate misinformation. This book is hoped to be one of many literature materials utilized by those seeking clarification in Black psychology. We hope that this book will propel future generations with a better sense of self.

Definitions

African Cosmology: A term coined by Dr. Kambon refers to African culture. Kambon believed that free expression is based on the African self-identification alignment to African culture.

Biases: Prejudice in favor of one thing or group over another, usually in the form of unfairness. It is also siding with someone or something through likeliness.

Black Psychology: The experience of African Americans emphasizing worldview and all that encompasses. This includes the value system, traditions, spirituality, sexuality, relationships, and social context of African Americans.

Blackness: The celebration of having African American DNA

Diagnostic and Statistical Manual of Mental Disorders (DSM-5): Diagnostic tool published by the American Psychological Association that professionals in the mental health field use.

De-Facto Segregation: Segregation that exists without the sanction of the law. This term describes the issue that legislation did not overtly segregate students by race, but school segregation continued.

Education Opportunity Program (EOP): An academic support system designed to help first-generation and low-income students succeed in college.

Examination for Professional Practice in Psychology (EPPP): A test requirement for psychology licensure within the United States of America.

Eugenics: Francis Galton coined the term Eugenics which meant "good stock" and meant that certain racial groups were superior to others.

Eurocentric Curriculum: Educational curriculum that is dominated by Eurocentric or Western knowledge. This education teaches African Americans, and other nonwhites that their ancestral history is not valuable enough to be taught in a classroom while showcasing that white history is highly favored and valuable enough for knowledge of all races and ethnicities.

Inequality: Unequal with status, rights, or opportunities.

Inequity: Lack of justice or fairness.

Informed Consent: The communication process between provider and client often leads to an agreement for care permission. It is also authorization granted by the person whose personal information is being extracted elsewhere. Typically this is utilized within a patient-doctor relationship but can be circumstantial in other predicaments.

Intergroup anxiety: Perceived negative stereotypes that can cause the ingroup to become anxious when around the outgroup.

Involuntary Whiteness: The bias of European standards forced upon African Americans and other non-whites through the societal system of systemic racism, which is forced acculturation, matriculated assimilation, white privilege, oppression, injustice, discrimination, and white supremacy.

Medical College Admission Test (MCAT): A mandated competency evaluation is utilized as a prerequisite before being accepted into medical school within the United States of America.

Psychologist: Doctorate level clinician who studies mental states, diagnoses, and conducts psychological assessments.

Psychiatrist: Medical Doctor clinician studies mental health and physical aspects of psychological problems and can prescribe psychotropic medications.

Stereotype threat: A situational circumstance where people feel themselves to be at risk of conforming to their social group's stereotype, and the term usually relates to academics.

Theoretical Orientation: Conceptual framework that clinicians utilize while conducting therapeutic services.

The Great Migration: The relocation of Blacks from the Southern to Northern states due to dissatisfactory economic opportunities and harsh segregationist laws.

Three-Fifths Compromise: Amendment verbalized that each enslaved African American counted as three/fifths of a person.

Whiteness: The way white people, their customs, and beliefs operate as the standard of which all other groups are compared or the infringement of this onto those who are not white.

White Psychology: A discipline of psychology that is not recognized but encompasses modern-day society as psychology is solely centralized around white people in all capacities.

References

Allison, K.W., & Belgrave, F.Z. (2018). *Introduction to African American Psychology.* Sage Publications, Inc. https://www.sagepub.com/sites/default/files/upm-binaries/93605_Chapter_1__Introduction_to_African_A merican_Psychology.pdf

American Psychological Association. (2017). *Demographic characteristics of APA members by membership characteristics.* https://www.apa.org/workforce/publications/17-member-profiles/table-1.pdf

American Psychological Association. (2012). Joseph White, PhD. https://www.apa.org/pi/oema/resources/ethnicity-health/psychologists/white#:~:text=Known%20as%20the%20%E2%80%9Cgodfather%20of,psychology%20from%20Michigan%20State%20University.

American Psychological Association. (n.d). *America's first black female psychologist.* Retrieved from http://www.apa.org/monitor/2008/11/prosser.aspx Stern, A.M. (2015). *Eugenic Nation: Faults and frontiers of better breeding in modern America.* University of California Press.

Baker, C.N. (2013). Social support and success in higher education: The influence of on-campus support on

African American and Latino college students. *The Urban Review, 45*(5), 632–650. https://doi-org.ezproxy.medaille.edu/10.1007/s11256-013-0234-9

Benjamin, L. T., Jr., Henry, K. D., & McMahon, L. R. (2005). Inez Beverly Prosser and the Education of African Americans. *Journal of the History of the Behavioral Sciences, 41(1),* 43–62. https://doi-org.ezproxy.medaille.edu/10.1002/jhbs.20058

Black Psychiatrists of America, Inc. | Washington, DC | Home. http://www.bpaincpsych.org/. Accessed 4 Jan. 2021.

Burris, J. L. (2012). On enhancing competent work with African American clients: *Challenging persistent racial disparity trends by examining the role of the working alliance. Journal of Applied Rehabilitation Counseling, 43*(3), 3–12. https://doi-org.ezproxy.medaille.edu/10.1891/0047-2220.43.3.3

Brantley, M. (2020, August 30). *Robert L. Williams II, Arkansas Native and Distinguished University Professor Who Coined Term 'Ebonics,' Dies at 90.* Arkansas Times. https://arktimes.com/arkansas-blog/2020/08/30/robert-l-williams-ii-arkansas-native-and-distinguished-university-professor-who-coined-term-Ebonics-dies-at-90

Chatterji, R. (2020, July 8). *Fighting Systemic Racism in K-12 Education: Helping Allies Move From the*

Keyboard to the School Board. Center for American Progress.
https://www.americanprogress.org/issues/education-k-12/news/2020/07/08/487386/fighting-systemic-racism-k-12-education-helping-allies-move-keyboard-school-board/

Clewell, B., & Anderson, B. (1995). *African Americans in Higher Education: An Issue of Access. Humboldt Journal of Social Relations, 21*(2), 55-79. Retrieved January 22, 2021, from http://www.jstor.org/stable/23263010

Council of National Psychological Associations for the Advancement of Ethnic Minority Interests. (2016). *Testing and assessment with persons & communities of color. Washington, DC: American Psychological Association.* Retrieved from https://www.apa.org/pi/oema

Curtis-Boles, H. (2017). Clinical strategies for working with clients of African descent. *Best Practices in Mental Health: An International Journal, 13*(2), 61–72.

Dr. Margaret Morgan Lawrence. (n.d.). *Changing the Fate of Medicine.* Retrieved January 3,2020 from https://cfmedicine.nlm.nih.gov/physicians/biography_19 5.html

Dictionary of American Negro Biography (New York: W.W. Norton and
Co., 1982); G. James Fleming and Christian E. Burckel, eds., *Who's Whoin Colored America* (New York: Christian E. Burckel & Associates,

1950).

Graves, S. L., Jr. (2009). Albert Sidney Beckham: The first African American school psychologist. *School Psychology International, 30*(1), 5–23. https://doi-org.ezproxy.medaille.edu/10.1177/0143034308101847

Gutenberg, P. (n.d.). Herman George Canady. Retrieved January 24, 2021, from http://self.gutenberg.org/articles/herman_george_canady *Health Matters: Stories of Science, Care & Wellness. It Happened Here: Dr. Margaret Morgan Lawrence.* (n.d). New York Presbyterian. https://healthmatters.nyp.org/happened-dr-margaret-morgan-lawrence/

Helfgott, E.A. (2018). *Jeanne Spurlock, M.D.(1921-199).* Black Past. https://www.blackpast.org/african-american-history/spurlock-jeanne-m-d-1921-1999/#:~:text=Jeanne%20Marybeth%20Spurlock%20was%20a,to%20win%20the%20Edward%20A.

Herman George Canady. (2020, September 13). *In Wikipedia.* https://en.wikipedia.org/wiki/Herman_George_Canady

Heung, C. (2008). *Solomon Carter Fuller (1872-1953).* Retrieved from https://www.blackpast.org/african-american-history/fuller-solomon-carter-1872-1953/ *History.com* editors. (2010, March 10). *The Great Migration.* History. *https://www.history.com/topics/black-history/great-migration*

History.com editors. (2018, March 8). *Tulsa Race Massacre.* History. https://www.history.com/topics/roaring-twenties/tulsa-race-massacre

Jewish Women's Archive. *"De facto segregation in the North: Introductory Essay."* (Viewed on January 3, 2021) <https://jwa.org/teach/livingthelegacy/de-facto-segregation-in-north-introductory-essay>.

Journal of the History of the Neurosciences 9:3 (2000); Carl C. Bell, "Solomon Carter Fuller: Where the Caravan Rested,"

Journal of American Medical Association 95:10 (2005); Rayford W. Logan and Michael R. Winston, eds.,

Kaiser Family Foundation. (2020). *Changes in Health Coverage by Race and Ethnicity since the ACA,* 2010-2018. Retrieved from https://www.kff.org/disparities-policy/issue-brief/changes-in-health-coverage-by-race-and-ethnicity-since-the-aca-2010-2018/

Kenneth Bancroft Clark 1914-2005. (2005). *The Journal of Blacks in Higher Education,* (48), 118-119. Retrieved December 17, 2020, from http://www.jstor.org/stable/25073259

Kobi Kambon. (2021, January 3). *In Wikipedia.* *https://en.wikipedia.org/wiki/Kobi_Kambon*

Kobi Kazembe Kalongi Kambon (aka Joseph A. Baldwin, PH.D). (n.d.). Florida Agricultural and Mechanical University. Retrieved January 21, 2021 from http://www.famu.edu/index.cfm?continuinged&Aboutthe 2010ConferenceHonoree

Lal, S. (2002). *Giving children security*: Mamie Phipps *Clark and the racialization of child psychology. American Psychologist, 57*(1), 20–28. https://doi-org.ezproxy.medaille.edu/10.1037/0003-066X.57.1.20

Mary Kaplan and Alfred R. Henderson, "Solomon Carter Fuller, M.D.
(1872-1953): *American Pioneer in Alzheimer's Disease Research,*"

Mental Divide: The Psychology Test That's Failing Minorities. (2019, December 9). OZY.
 https://www.ozy.com/the-new-and-the-next/mental-divide-the-qualifying-test-thats-twice-as-hard-for-minority-psychologists/96496/

Mental Health America. (2020). *Black And African American Communities And Mental Health.* Retrieved from
https://www.mhanational.org/issues/black-and-african-american-communities-and-mental-health

Mohammed, H. *Recognizing African-American contributions to neurology: The role of Solomon Carter Fuller (1872-1953)* in Alzheimer's disease research. *Alzheimer's Dement.* 2020; 1- 5. https://doi.org/10.1002/alz.12183

(n.d.). Retrieved January 24, 2021, from https://psychology.okstate.edu/museum/afroam/bio.html
(n.d.). Retrieved January 24, 2021, from https://myemail.constantcontact.com/Empowering-Minds-February-Newsletter%E2%80%93Famous-African-American-Psychologists%E2%80%93V-Day-Tips%E2%80%93and-More%E2%80%93.html?soid=1123708538063&aid=thVKPBtOF_0

National Institute for Education Statistics. (2015). *Public School Safety and Discipline: 2013-2014.* Institute of Education Sciences. https://nces.ed.gov/pubs2015/2015051.pdf

New Study Shows EPPP Can Discriminate Against African-Americans, Hispanics. (2018, December 18). The Psychology Times. Retrieved January 23, 2020 from https://thepsychologytimes.com/2018/12/18/new-study-shows-eppp-can-discriminate-against-african-americans-hispanics/

Perry, Andre M. *"For Better Student Outcomes, Hire More Black Teachers." Brookings*, Brookings, 16 Oct. 2019, https://www.brookings.edu/blog/brown-center-chalkboard/2019/10/16/for-better-student-outcomes-hire-more-black-teachers/.

Pickren, W. E., & Tomes, H. (2002). The legacy of Kenneth B Clark to the APA: The Board of Social and Ethical Responsibility for Psychology. *American Psychologist, 57*(1), 51–59.

https://doi-org.ezproxy.medaille.edu/10.1037/0003-066X.57.1.51

Psychology's Feminist Voice. (n.d.). *Inez Beverly Prosser.*
https://feministvoices.com/profiles/inez-beverly-prosser
Race-based legislation. (n.d.). Retrieved January 24, 2021, from
https://www.pbs.org/wgbh/aia/part4/4p2957.html

"Racism Fuels Poor Mental Health Outcomes for Black Students." Inside Higher Ed | Higher Education News, Career Advice, Jobs,
https://www.insidehighered.com/news/2020/10/23/racism-fuels-poor-mental-health-outcomes-black-students. Accessed 27 Jan. 2021.

Runes, C. (2019, February 26). *Following a long history, the 2020 Census risks undercounting the black population.* Retrieved January 23, 2021, from https://www.urban.org/urban-wire/following-long-history-2020-census-risks-undercounting-black-population

Sawyer, T. F. (2000, May). *Francis Cecil Sumner: His views and influence on African American higher education.*
http://commons.trincoll.edu/macecourses/files/2016/11/Sumner_2000.pdf
Sharpless, B.A. (2019). *Are demographic Variables Associated with Performance on the Examination for Professional Practice in Psychology (EPPP)?* J Psychol.153(2):161-172.   doi:

10.1080/00223980.2018.1504739. Epub 2018 Oct 22. PMID: 30346907.

Social Science Space. (2017, December 5). *The Godfather of Black Psychology: Joseph White, 1932-2017.* https://www.socialsciencespace.com/2017/12/godfather-black-psychology-joseph-white-1932-2017/

Stern, A. M. (2015). *Eugenic Nation: Faults and Frontiers of Better Breeding in Modern America.* Berkeley: University of California Press.

Stuart, R. (2018, January 2). *Celebrating the Life of Dr. Joseph L. White.* Diverse; Issues in Higher Education. https://diverseeducation.com/article/107713/

The British Psychology Society. (2020, October 9). *They taught integrity: The lives of Francis Sumner and Inez Beverley Prosser.* .https://www.bps.org.uk/blogs/black-history-month/they-taught-integrity-francis-sumner-inez-beverley-prosser

The Association of Black Psychologists – Just Another WordPress Site. https://abpsi.org/. Accessed 4 Jan. 2021.

The Impact of the Brown v. Board of Education Decision on Postsecondary Participation of African Americans. Harvey, William B.; Harvey, Adia M.; King, Mark, 2004 Team, G. (2011, November 11). *Inez Beverly Prosser (1895-1934).* https://www.goodtherapy.org/famous-psychologists/inez-beverly-prosser.html

They taught integrity: the lives of Francis Sumner and Inez Beverley Prosser (2020, October 9). Retrieved January 22, 2021 from https://www.bps.org.uk/blogs/black-history-month/they-taught-integrity-francis-sumner-inez-beverley-prosser

Thomas, R. K. (2012). Sumner, Francis Cecil. In Encyclopedia of the history of psychological theories 0fol. 2, pp. 1049-1050. New York, NY: Springer-Verlag

Trailblazing University of Cincinnati *Alumna to Be Honored at April Symposium.* (2008, Mar 03). *US Fed News Service, Including US State News.* Retrieved from

http://search.proquest.com/docview/469501400?accounti d=1229

Teamcassius. "BLACKIPEDIA: Who Is Robert Lee Williams II?" *Cassius*, Cassius | Born Unapologetic | News, Style, Culture, 29 Mar. 2020, cassiuslife.com/92222/who-is-robert-lee-williams-ii/.

"The Diversity Gap in Medicine and How the MCAT Shaped It | AUA." Https://www.Auamed.Org/, https://www.auamed.org/blog/diversity-gap-medicine-mcat-shaped/. Accessed 4 Jan. 2021.

U.S. Census Bureau. (2012). Profile America facts for features—Asian/ Pacific American heritage month: May 2012. Retrieved from http://www.census.gov/newsroom/releases/archives/facts_for_f eatures_special_editions/cb12-ff09.html.

Wallace, B. (2015, February 28). *10 African and African American Psychologists You Should Know. Active Minds.* https://www.activeminds.org/blog/10-african-african-american-psychologists-you-should-know/

Wallace, B. C. (2008). *Toward equity in health: A new global approach to health disparities* (B. C. Wallace (Ed.)). Springer Publishing Company.

Why the Academic Achievement Gap is a Racist Idea – AAIHS. (2016, October 20).Aaihs.org.https://www.aaihs.org/why-the-academic-achievement-gap-is-a-racist-idea/

Williams, R. L., Dotson, W., Dow, P., & Williams, W. S. (1980). The war against testing: A current status report. *Journal of Negro Education*, 49, 263–273.

Wirga, Mariusz & Debernardi, Michael & Wirga, Aleksandra. (2018). Our Memories of Maxie C. Maultsby Jr. 1932–2016. *Journal of Rational-Emotive & Cognitive-Behavior Therapy.* 37. 10.1007/s10942-018-0309-3.

About the Authors

Tamera Gittens was born in Brooklyn, New York, on July 5, 1994, enveloped by her family's Trinidadian culture. Tamera was first introduced to the mental health field at the age of 15 when she obtained a job at Downstate Hospital with her father through the Summer Youth Employment Program (SYEP). She worked on the hospital's psychiatric floor and was tasked with handing out ice cups throughout the day, checking in with the patients, and a great deal of administrative work. During her time there, she tried her best to check in with each patient at least once a day and found that many patients had a mouthful of stories to tell her as they began to notice her check-ins were routine. She became fascinated learning about each patient's diagnosis through their charts. She also noticed that the psychiatrist visited once a week, prescribed medication, and left so there was no actual therapy being provided to the patients. Essentially there was a great disregard for the positive effects of therapy in conjunction with medication. Through these observations, it was evident that these patients were not learning any coping skills for everyday life after their discharge. During this time, Tamera realized she wanted to obtain a job in the mental health field, providing therapy to minorities. Tamera attended Clara Barton High School, where she graduated with a Medical Assistant certification after two years of clinical rotations at Kings County Hospital. She obtained her Bachelor's degree in Forensic Psychology at John Jay College and then obtained her Master's degree in School Counseling at New York University. She worked as a School Counselor at a middle school for three years, where she advocated for students to help eliminate all barriers to ensure positive and successful school years. Through social-emotional, academic, and career development, she helped her students excel and reach their full potential right in time for high school. She is currently at Medaille College finishing up her second Master's degree in Mental Health Counseling and works as a Behavior Specialist, identifying and assisting individuals and families in accessing needed preventive and primary health care services as well as evaluating patient outcomes and progress toward achieving objectives and goals of the care plan. Tamera's passion and drive has only increased as she works in the field, creating a safe space for Black narratives in therapy.

About the Authors

Nicól Osborne was born in Brooklyn, New York, on January 8, 1994. She is of Trinidadian and Grenadian descent. Nicól was first introduced to the mental health field as a child; her favorite show was "House". While Dr. House was a genius medical doctor, his personality was self-destructive, and that fascinated Nicól that he could be analytical and logical but extremely unstable. During 11th and 12th grade, Nicól went to a vocational school named BOCES. While there, the curriculum was centralized around learning about patient nursing skills, mental and overall health. External clinical rotations were conducted coupled with internal labs with manikins learning how to be hands-on from vitals, venipuncture, proper PPE, hygienic protocols and other wide range of nursing skills. Nicól obtained her medical assistant certification at the end of the program. She went on to major in Nursing in college but after taking a psychology elective, switched her major and has remained a psychology major moving forward. Nicol obtained two Associate degrees; A.S in Pre Med Biology and A.A in Psychology at OCCC. Nicól obtained her Bachelor's degree in Forensic Psychology at John Jay College and then obtained her Master's degree in Social Work at Fordham University. Nicól is currently working on a PsyD doctorate in clinical psychology at Southern California University. She worked as a Social Worker for three years at JASA; in a community guardianship program under Article 81 guardianship laws appointed by the Supreme Court in Manhattan, NY. Her duties consisted of an in-home and in-office assessment of adult clients' social and emotional needs with the assistance of other social work and/or other professional consultants. She conducted individual and family counseling and guidance in resolving the client's problems. Nicól is currently working as a Researcher helping with the COVID-19 pandemic and as a Therapist. She is currently obtaining her predoctoral hours (Practicum and Internship) in Hawaii; she hopes to conduct her postdoctoral hours there as well.

A STORM OF LOVE

The Storm Series
Book 2

Terri Brisbin

A Storm of Love

ISBN: 978-0-9985326-9-1

Book Cover Design: © Carrie Divine of Seductive Designs
Photo copyright © Period Images
Photo copyright: © Sandralise/Depositphotos.com
Photo copyright: © gvictoria/Depositphotos.com

Print Formatting: Nina Pierce of Seaside Publications

This dark, emotional and steamy fantasy romance series set in medieval Scotland was previously published by Kensington Books in their Brava imprint and is now re-released by the author.

Luckenbooth
Press

A Storm of Passion – Book 1

Connor has the ability to see the past, present and future and uses his gift for the benefit of his wealthy patron. But, it comes at a high price—his power first blinds him and then will kill him … if the woman intent on his death doesn't get to him first. She claims he killed her family, but he only knows relief and pleasure when she is with him.

Moira has lived to avenge her family's destruction that the Seer caused. But captured and made his prisoner, she discovers he is not what he seems and so much more. As she watches his dark power control him, Moira also finds a sensuality that draws her closer and closer and tempts her to put aside her vengeance.

As darkness and danger gather around them and the curse of his Fae father reaches its deadly conclusion, will Connor and Moira find the love that could save them both?

"Boldly sensual and richly emotional." *Booklist*

"Hot and compelling!" NYT Bestselling Author Madeline Hunter

A Storm of Love – Book 2

Agneis of Mull betrayed the Fae prince who loved her and lost everything and everyone. Exiled for her sins to the untamed lands of Argyll, a chance encounter with a younger man offer Agneis the possibility of a new life … and love.

Breac never expected someone like Agneis to come into his life, but he saves her life even as she saves his soul. Can their love, one based on passion, stand against old enemies who now threaten and a dangerous curse of the Fae?

A Storm of Pleasure – Book 3

Katla Svensdottir will do anything to save her brother from death— even give herself to the man they call the Truthsayer for his pleasure. For, unless Gavin of Orkney reveals his innocence, her brother will be executed for treason. And sharing this man's bed will not be a hardship for her, even if she pays a dear price later.

Gavin needs Katla to ease the incessant and maddening noise in his head and he promises her anything to get her to agree to help him—even to help her brother. But, Gavin already knows the boy's truth and played a part in his arrest and his father's death.

When kings and powerful men fight over Gavin's extraordinary gift and when the truth will reveal too many dark and dangerous secrets, will Katla be his salvation or his executioner?

"Brisbin's A STORM OF PLEASURE is fast-paced and wildly hot with a touch of the supernatural." --*RT Book Reviews*

Mistress of the Storm – Book 4

Duncan of Skye heals with his touch and many powerful nobles vie to use it for themselves. But every use of his power brings pain and destroys his body and he knows he will not survive much longer. When a woman given to him gives him blessed relief from his suffering, he knows he must keep her as he seeks a way to end the curse.

Isabel has been forced by her stepfather to use her body for his aims. She's learned to numb herself as she is given to many men to serve as his spy and blackmailer. But, when she is sold to the man called the Healer, she finds him to be different than any other before him.

Time is running out for Duncan and, as he draws Isabel closer and closer, they discover that they could be each other's redemption or their destruction. When love could break the curse can these two risk everything and claim it?

"A passionate and powerful page-turner!"
— NYT Bestselling Author Teresa Medeiros

"Explicit love scenes and emotional turmoil lend drama en route to a powerfully moving conclusion." — *Publisher's Weekly*

"MISTRESS OF THE STORM is a scorching romance! Emotionally riveting and powerfully passionate, this book is a fantastic read!" – *The Romance Reviews*

*Top Pick July 2011 and Best Book in Erotic-Historical Fantasy Romance of 2011 by *The Romance Reviews*

USA TODAY BESTSELLING
AUTHOR

TERRI
BRISBIN

THE STORM SERIES

A STORM OF
LOVE

One

Near Kilmartin Glen, southwest Scotland, 1083 A.D.

Breac peered up at the darkening sky and wiped the rain out of his face. For the fifth time in only minutes. The storm swirled, throwing winds in his face and dowsing him in waves of rain that soaked through the layers of woolen plaid. His chances and plans of returning to his home in less than three days faded even as the daylight did. Hell!

His luck in finding the healer near Dunadd had been unexpected, for 'twas rumored that she traveled through the Highlands during the summer months, gathering plants and seedlings for use in her concoctions. He reached down and touched the pouch tied carefully to his belt. Concoctions such as the one he now carried back to heal his sister from the strange, lingering fever that struck her down.

Pushing on through the boggy ground, Breac tried to force his way along the washed-out path, but his steps became slower and slower. The unrelenting rain would, he feared, be his undoing this day. Finally, accepting the futility of making it any farther before night fell completely, he began to search for a dry, or drier, place to seek refuge from this storm. He spied a clearing ahead and made his way there, hoping to be able to see more once he reached it. Just as he approached it, Breac reached up to push a low-hanging branch from his path and stopped, searching for a good place to seek protection from the storm on this higher ground.

A copse of trees with thick and heavily leafed branches offered him exactly what he needed. Without heavy brush at their base, the canopy they formed above the ground would keep him mostly dry. Creeping in between the trunks, he kicked the pile of damp leaves from beneath him and slid down, using one of the trees at his back as a guide. With his tightly woven wool cloak wrapped around him, Breac might keep the worst of the storm away. Some time passed as he dozed in and out of a light, fitful sleep, one filled with dreams, nay nightmares, of his sister's death.

Breac reached up and rubbed his face, frustration and sadness filling him once more at the thought of his failure. Fenella was his responsibility. He'd sworn to his mother that he would care for her and protect her, and instead, he'd failed. Releasing a deep breath, he knew

Terri Brisbin

that he was her only hope now and he would not fail her
again. When the rain began to ease a bit, he thought about
getting a few more miles behind him, but the winds did
not relent and without the light of the moon, it would be
impossible to see his path until morn.

Leaning his head back against the tree's trunk behind
him, he closed his eyes and sought sleep once more. No
more than several minutes could have passed when the
sounds of someone approaching grew louder ... and
closer. Others traveling in this same dismal weather? He
knew not, but decided to stay in his place and let them
pass, if they did, without bringing attention to himself.

Two men, riding horses, broke through the last of the
bushes surrounding this clearing and stopped. One of
them, the younger one by looks, lifted a large bundle
from his lap and dropped it on the ground. The sounds
made when it hit the ground told him that it was alive.

An animal of some kind? Breac slowly pulled himself
up to stand, but stayed within the protection of the trees
as he watched the younger man climb down from his
horse and push the bundle with his foot. It rolled several
times as he kicked it across the clearing to the brush at
the edge. A cry or grunt echoed with each kick. Breac
waited.

"Are ye awake then?" the man asked as he reached
down and, using his dagger, slit open the cloak or sack
that enshrouded the person within. He gripped both sides
and tore it, pulling it free and dumping a bound, naked

3

woman on the wet ground.

A woman? Aye, clearly one, whose feminine curves were not hidden by gown or cloak. Gagged, with her hands tied behind her back, she struggled weakly against those bonds.

"Go ahead, Keegan," the older man called out from his place on top of his horse. "Finish this."

From the seriousness of the tone used when giving the order, Breac expected the younger man to kill the woman, but the younger one put his dagger back in his boot and held out his hand. The older one tossed a large cudgel to him. Rolling her on her back with his foot, he positioned himself over the woman and lifted the club.

"This time you should heed his warning and not return to the village," he said swinging the heavy weapon over his head. The woman began to struggle under his foot and he leaned more heavily on her until she stopped. "This time, you will not be able to come back."

Breac was within an arm's reach before he even decided to intervene, grabbing the club from the young man and throwing it into the trees. He took hold of this Keegan's cloak and tossed him aside, away from the woman, where he could watch both of the men.

"You should not interfere in something not of your concern, stranger," the older man warned. "Her lord has exiled her and she disobeys his orders. He has the right to punish her and we carry out his orders."

Breac could not think of whose lands were nearby or

which lord would order such a thing, but he shook his head.

"Who orders such a thing?" he asked. Glancing over at her was a mistake as he realized in a second for her eyes were wild with terror and her naked body shook in fear and cold. "I see not the brand of a whore on her breast. No fingers or hands are missing befitting a thief. What crime has she committed against her lord to earn this kind of punishment?"

He knew he had no standing, no legal right to stop their actions, and he had no doubt they did act on the orders of their lord. But something in her gaze drew him into this and forced him to step where he most likely should not go. The two drew swords then and faced him, one on foot, one on horse, and he knew he was no match for them. But he stood his ground, keeping them on one side and her on the other. Needing to ease the situation or end up dead like this unknown woman would be, Breac held his hands up to show he was not going to fight them.

"It seems a waste of an able-bodied woman when I need a slave to work my farm," he said. Nodding at her, he made his offer. "I will take her and make certain she never returns here." He tugged at his belt and breeches with an obvious gesture, leered at her nakedness, and then smiled. "She will not have the strength to go very far when I finish with her."

The men understood his meaning and so did the

woman, for she struggled once more against the ropes binding her legs and hands, managing only to dig herself deeper into the layer of mud at the edge of the clearing where she lay. He could see the doubt in their expressions but he waited, not offering any more words that could sway them or seem overly anxious. He only hoped, for some reason not clear to even him, that the look of disdain for their assignment and exhaustion on the man's face won out over any qualms of handing her over to him. Finally, the older one nodded.

"Take her then and make certain she is never seen any farther south than the standing stones again." He pointed off to the south toward the rings of ancient stone pillars that stood like silent sentinels along the glen. So, her lord governed the lands south of Dunadd then? Breac nodded, but Keegan objected.

"How do we know he will keep his word, Callum? If she returns, it will be our backs that will bear the whip. I say we at least do what our lord ordered—break her legs to make certain she cannot come closer than this." He put his sword back in the scabbard but picked up a large rock as his weapon.

Holy Christ in Heaven! Breaking her legs as he intended to do was as much a death sentence as simply killing her. She would never walk again and the wounds would no doubt fester. Her end would be tortuous and filled with fever and grievous pain. What sin could she have committed to warrant such a brutal punishment? He

appealed to Callum, hoping the older warrior would agree.

"I have nothing to give you but my word and I give that as my solemn oath. This woman will never return here or any place south of the stones."

She whimpered again, but he would not look at her. Meeting Callum's gaze, he waited for his answer. He would deal with her once these men were on their way.

"Where is your farm, stranger?" Callum asked.

"More than three days walk from here, many miles north and east of An t-Oban Lotharnach," he exaggerated, wanting the soldier to be comforted by such a distance. He thought Callum would not agree, but then he called Keegan off and the younger man dropped the rock and returned to his horse, muttering his unhappiness with every step. Breac held his breath, hoping this tentative agreement would stand. Callum leaned over and said something under his breath to Keegan, the words he could not hear but they seemed to quiet his objections.

"She is yours now," Callum called out. "Stand by your word or I will find you."

He watched as they left the clearing, heading back in the direction from which they'd come. He didn't move until the sounds of their departure disappeared into the sounds of the storm around him. Any daylight faded quickly and he must handle her before it was too dark to see anything.

Breac reached down and drew his own dagger from

its place in his boot and walked toward her. She struggled now, but could not go anywhere but deeper into the mud tied as she was. He stood over her and shook his head in disgust. Then, with blade in hand, he bent down.

Two

She could only hope it would be a quicker death than the one Donnell had ordered for her. Aigneis had no chance against this giant of a man, not trussed as she was and exhausted from the brutal ride to wherever this place was. Donnell had claimed to love her and to accept her but now he ordered her death without a moment's hesitation. To fit his needs and to accomplish his goals.

Offering up a prayer to the Christian God, for the old ones had long ignored her pleas, she closed her eyes and waited for the dagger to do its work. After committing as many sins as she had, it did not surprise her that no god would help her. The prick of the dagger into her skin as it sliced through the rough ropes at her ankles shocked more than hurt her.

Aigneis opened her eyes to find the man reaching for her now. Ah, his promise to use her would happen before he killed her and to do that her legs needed to be freed.

Unable to watch, she closed her eyes tightly and tried not to struggle and make him angry. Angry men were more dangerous and more likely to add pain to the punishments they wrought. Keegan was one of such men.

Yet again, his actions surprised her, for instead of spreading her legs, he grabbed her at the waist and turned her. When she thought he would position himself at her back and take her from behind, the prick of the dagger scratched her skin again, this time at her wrists. Her hands and arms were without feeling from being tied so tightly for so long and fell useless at her sides. She could not even lift them to defend herself now.

The man rolled her onto her back once more and just as he reached for the thick gag stuffed into her mouth, her arms and hands burned with feeling again. Like a fire racing through her body, her skin and muscles came alive again and she moaned against the rough cloth at the intense pain of it. Before she knew it, the dagger sliced again and he tugged the cloth out of her mouth.

Why did he draw this out? Why did he not simply strike and end it? His touch was almost gentle as he lifted her muddy hair from her face and touched the place across her cheeks and mouth where the cloth had been tied so tightly. This was worse than pain or facing his anger, for it made her damned soul think there was still a chance for life. And there could not be that.

Or could there?

He seemed neither inclined to take her body or her life

just then. Once he'd released all the bonds, he stood and lifted her slowly to her feet, supporting her from behind with his strong arms around her. The mud made his efforts more difficult and he stilled for a moment when one of his hands slipped along her skin and cupped her breast instead. Waiting for the inevitable, Aigneis could not believe when he moved his hand back to her waist and stood with her.

"You must move around," he said, his voice gruff with the effort it was taking him to hold her up. "The ropes could have damaged your limbs and lying on the cold ground will not help." When his hand slipped a second time and he let out a harsh curse, Aigneis flinched and waited for him to strike. Instead he placed his large hands around her arms like the gold cuffs she used to wear when she was … She shook her head to try to clear her thoughts.

He stood at least a foot taller than she and, because of the hooded cloak or cloth he wore, she only caught a glimpse of his true appearance. With the rain and wind blowing in her eyes, she could only hear his voice and feel the strength in his arms as they held her and in his legs as they supported her.

He began walking forward, forcing her legs to move. She wanted to curse him for it as the painful burning crept down now to her feet, making every step an anguishing one. They'd struggled through more than a dozen paces before the pain lessened and her legs began

to support more of her weight. Just as she was able to take a few steps on her own, she felt her body tumbling down. Her scream echoed through the trees.

The icy cold of the water as she hit forced her breath from her body and it surrounded her, pulling her under and down. Aigneis struggled against the cold and the water, trying to hold her breath as she fought to find her way out. Did he mean to drown her like some unwanted dog? Her flailing hands grasped onto his strong arm in that instant and instead of holding her down, he pulled her above the surface. Gasping, she clung to his arm, hoping to get a chance to fight back.

"Hush now," he said softly as he lifted her out of the water. "You were caked with mud and bleeding from a wound I could not see." He smoothed her hair back out of her eyes, treating her with a gentleness that belied her new position—slave to him as master.

"Are you going to kill me?" she asked, trying to calm both the fear and the awful coldness that now shot through her.

He released her with a dark frown and fumbled in the leather bag he carried over his shoulder for something. She drew back as far as she could, but his tall form blocked her way. With the stream at her back and trees forming a row on either side of them, she stood trapped within his grasp. Instead of a weapon, he drew out a garment and shook it out.

"Wring the water out of your hair and put this on," he

ordered. "Though 'tis summer and the air can warm, that stream starts high in the hills and never does."

It was a tunic, a long one that ended at her knees when she managed to get it over her head, after twisting her hair to release as much water as possible. The front gaped, exposing her breasts and much of her stomach to his gaze. Since he'd seen and touched her naked body both covered in mud and clean, she thought that was the least of her troubles.

Until she noticed the glint of lust in his gaze as he pushed the woolen cloak from his head and stared at her. 'Twas almost as though covering some of her nakedness was more appealing to him than seeing every inch of her skin. It lasted only a few moments, before he swallowed and nodded at the sky.

"We have precious little daylight left. We should see to your leg and find a drier place for the night." His voice was even and almost comforting. He held out his hand as he backed a few paces from her. "Come."

Whether the exhaustion of the last weeks finally took control or the insanity that Donnell accused her of having set in, she knew not. Aigneis knew only that she could fight no longer. She met the man's gaze as he nodded and motioned with his hand to follow him. Lowering her eyes, she now noticed the gash on her leg and watched as the blood trickled down over her ankle and dripped onto the already-soaked ground beneath her.

She knew not if the storm had strengthened around

her, but her sight grew dark and hazy and her ears buzzed like the time a swarm of bees had attacked her. Squinting, Aigneis noticed that the man seemed farther away and ... grayer, as if all the color had left his hair, his eyes, his skin.

"Do not."

His voice stern now, he warned her against ... something. Shaking her head in confusion, she felt as though back in the stream with the water rising around her. She reached out her hand in his direction, hoping he would pull her from death once more, but her world went black before he could.

Her pale face turned ghostly white and her eyes rolled back into her head. Breac tried to get her attention when he noticed the changes begin, understanding what would happen next, but she lost consciousness as he watched. Lucky for her, he needed to take but one step to catch her before she landed in the mud again. He leaned over and scooped her into his arms while yet trying to figure out the reasons for his actions of the last several minutes.

Breac carried her back to the clearing and sought out the rough shelter of the copse where he'd left most of his provisions. Holding her slight form against his chest, he eased back down to sit on the ground. Once there, he tugged most of the length of his woolen cloak from around him and wrapped it around her. Then, as the last rays of the storm-covered sun faded, he shifted her in his arms and waited for her to wake. He must have drifted

into sleep for the next thing he knew, she scrambled away from him, dragging his cloak with her. The other trees acted as a boundary and when she reached them, she could go no farther.

He stood then, stretched his arms and legs to get rid of the stiffness from sitting too still for too long, and searched his sack for his flint and the few pieces of dry kindling he always carried. Without a fire he could not see her in the darkness. Or more importantly it seemed, she could not see him. He could hear her terror in the rate of her breathing.

"I will try to start a fire," he explained. "Stay where you are."

Breac ignored the sounds of distress from her and got some of the kindling burning. With that faint light, he was able to find some drier branches and start them to burn. They didn't need a fire for the whole night, just long enough for him to see to her wounds and for them to settle in. Everything else could be managed in daylight, hopefully a drier one than this one had been. It took a short time, but soon he had a fire burning well enough to see their small shelter.

And the woman.

She sat huddled against a tree, wrapped in his cloak, watching every move he made. Her pale-colored eyes were wide with fear and she worried her teeth over the fullness of her bottom lip every time he gazed at her. Though her skin was the color of the pearls that his lord's

wife wore in a necklace, he knew from seeing her naked that it bore darkening bluish-purple bruises that had not yet shown their true color or size. It was her hair that fascinated him though, the hue of burnished silver with flecks of some darker shade through it. And, cut off as it was only a few inches from her scalp, it began to curl as it dried.

Breac's body reacted then, remembering on its own the pleasing shapes and softness of her body and ignoring the clear signs that she was older than him. Desire at this time was unseemly, even for a man who'd not had a woman in many weeks.

He crouched down, searching in his bag for the oatcakes and cheese he carried. Finding it he broke them in two and held out a portion of each to her. Trying to banish the desire that flowed through his blood now, he turned away after she took the food from his hand. That she took the food and then shifted back as far as she could bothered him in some deep way.

Breac waited for her to eat the cheese and then handed her a skin filled with ale. She accepted it the same way she accepted the food—a quick grab for it and then out of arm's reach. The action should not surprise him; it was an act of fear and, after witnessing what must be only a small part of the treatment she'd received from the men and their lord, it was one he could understand. So, like gentling a wild animal, he would accustom her to his presence. At least for the night.

He had no inclination to bring her to his home and his farm, no matter what story he told to get her released to him. The tasks of seeing to his sister and overseeing his own land and those that his lord owned were too important to be distracted by this woman. No matter that her gaze held a measure of pleading in it each time she looked at him, and no matter that his blood stirred for her in a way he'd not felt for a woman in a long, long time.

So wrapped in his own thoughts and his own arguments about her fate that he did not notice her approach, he startled when she held the skin out to him from just a foot or two away.

"My thanks," she whispered, as she stepped away once more.

"Come closer," he said. "The flame is meager and you cannot feel its heat from over there."

He watched as she stood, wrapped his cloak more securely around her body, and then took a hesitant step forward. She silently slid to sit nearer to the small sputtering fire, but remained as far from him as she could. The night had fallen deeply around them, the sounds of rain grew fainter as the minutes passed in silence. Putting the skin up to his mouth, he drank a mouthful before meeting her gaze.

"What are you called?" he asked.

The low flames sputtered and crackled and he waited for her to answer. What surprised him was the tone of her voice when she did speak.

"Aigneis," she said. Her voice was deeper than when she was terrified and her name flowed like the melody of some unsung song, touching something deep within him. Heat and warmth and comfort flowed through him in that moment, with just one word.

Her name.

"Say it again," he found himself almost pleading to hear it again.

Three

"My name is Aigneis."

Her exhaustion lulled her into revealing her name and, worse, it came out in that voice. The one she kept hidden from everyone. One of the few remnants of her time in the land of the sith, it had the most unusual effect on others, especially men. This time was no different. Her captor shifted as he sat on the ground and his eyes glimmered in response.

Aigneis cleared her throat and pitched her voice a bit, nearly whispering now so that it was not as evident. It was the reason the men assigned by her husband kept her gagged—he knew its effect and had warned them. She could, he claimed, tempt the angels from the heights of heaven to the depths of hell with that voice. And though it had tempted him to many, many things, he believed she could overpower the will of men and bend them to her bidding. 'Twas not true, but it did not stop him from

believing it or from spreading it as truth and making his people fear her.

"Where are you from?" Breac asked, his eyes intent on hers as he did, as though he was anxious to hear her speak.

Mayhap he was?

Uncertain about revealing anything else to him, she looked away, hoping in each second that passed that he would not challenge her silence. She watched as he lifted the skin to his mouth and drank from it another time. Just as she thought he would not speak again and as the pain in her body from being manhandled for days reached a level that made it impossible to ignore, his strong voice called out to her.

"I am called Breac," he said. He leaned toward the flames, revealing more of his face to her.

In addition to the strength in his voice and in his body, his face was chiseled by masculine angles, with a straight jaw and nose that showed a previous break. Instead of making him look weak, it added a sort of dangerous appeal to his looks. The thing about him that shocked her the most was his age.

Aigneis had lived almost thirty years, but this Breac appeared to be at least five or mayhap even seven years her younger. He wore his black, shoulder-length hair pulled away and tied at his neck. His beard was trimmed close, unlike most men who let their beards grow wild and bushy. But it was his eyes that caught her attention.

Not that their dark brown color was anything apart from ordinary. Nay, 'twas not their color, but the stark sorrow that lay deep within them when he was not paying attention to hiding it. The sorrow was so strong and so clear that it made her heart, one scarred by deception, betrayal, and loss, hurt at the sight of it. Aigneis held out her hand for the skin, thirsty from so many hours without nourishment or drink.

"What are your plans for me?" she asked softly. She did not wait for his reply, for her thirst threatened to overwhelm her, as did the pain piercing through her body and the exhaustion. Tipping it back, she drank several mouthfuls before realizing how little was still left and stopped. "Am I your slave now?"

She watched as a shiver pulsed through him and lust shone once more in his gaze, but only for a moment before he controlled it and banished it.

"I need no slave," he answered. "Come morning, I will take you farther north and release you."

Of all the things she expected and steeled herself to hear, that was not one of them. Did he speak the truth? Would he chance her going back to her ... lord and bearing such retribution from Donnell's men? As though she'd spoken her word aloud, he shook his head.

"I know not what happened to bring you here," he began. "And in such condition"—he paused, throwing a glance at her cropped hair and his clothing—"but you would be wise to seek a new place and a new life, far

from whichever lord you offended."

Considering how many she'd offended in her life, his advice was both warranted and wise, but he had no idea. Even her lord husband, who'd married her because of the bargain her father struck upon her return from the land of the sith, had no idea. 'Twas the chest filled with an unimagined wealth in gold that convinced her father and her husband to uphold their betrothal and to keep her. Until now.

Her body grew heavy even as her heart did when she dared to think of her ultimate sin. However, she knew this pain was from the beatings and the torturous ride here, bound and held on the back of a horse. She was about to ask his leave to sleep when he spoke again.

"Let me see to that gash and then seek your rest," he said. "The rain is letting up and I will leave at first light." The deep sorrow filled his gaze once more, yet unlike when lust crept in, he made no attempt to hide or banish it.

Aigneis handed the skin back to him, sliding back a few feet. His care was quick and efficient and soon the wound on her leg was clean and wrapped. Then she lay down on her side and curled in a ball. The woolen cloak wrapped around her smelled of his scent—masculine, leather, and something else—and she tried to stay awake long enough to watch him, yet uncertain of his plans. But the heaviness in her body and heart and soul took control and dragged her into a fitful sleep.

Sometime in the night, she awoke, whether from the cool air that settled around them making her shiver or his voice, she knew not. Breac mumbled in his sleep, his words sounded like prayers.

Prayers for Fenella. Fear that she could die. Fear that she would die before his return. All repeated over and over, disturbing his sleep but not waking him. Was Fenella his wife? She suffered from some illness and his guilt was clear from his words. Was this something from his past or the reason for his journey and his haste? He settled deeper into sleep as she thought on calling his name to rouse him from it.

Then later, as she shivered against the cold, Aigneis began to wake. Before she could force herself to sit up and wrap the cloak anew in hopes of better protection from the cold, she was surrounded by a soothing and comforting heat. Lulled back into sleep, she did not remember hearing anything else until his voice called her name again.

"Aigneis," he said. "You must wake now."

Only on his second call did she realize that he spoke her name and that his voice came from behind her. Startled that he was so close, she opened her eyes and tried to sit up. His weight on the cloak yet wrapped around her stopped her. His arm, resting across her waist, held her in place. His warm breath on the back of her neck teased her body and she shivered against it.

He lay next to her! Aigneis began to push him away,

but he clutched her tighter.

"Hush now," he whispered against her ear. "You lay shivering in the night and I thought to ease your discomfort." Breac lifted his arm once she stilled and then rolled to his feet away from her. "And to keep myself warmed as well," he admitted.

Aigneis scrambled to the other side of their small enclosure and tugged the cloak loose. Pushing her hair out of her face, she realized that he stared at her. His shirt gaped open again, this time though the bruises that covered her skin were visible to both of them in spite of the day's weak light.

Gathering the edges together, she stood and picked up the cloak once more, her body aching with every move she made. Before she could even try to replace the cloak over herself, he took it from her and wrapped it around her shoulders.

"See to your needs at the stream." His voice was brusque. "I ... we have a good distance to travel before night."

Aigneis did not argue or even comment, she simply followed his instructions and walked away from their shelter, back through the trees where he pointed. With each step her feet and legs screamed and her back tightened in pain. Her mind had lost the ability to make plans and she only knew she would not lie down and die here as Donnell had ordered and hoped. She must live. She must live to seek her sons.

Breac tried to focus on the tasks he needed to complete in order to get on the road, but his gaze followed the injured woman as she walked away. He'd seen the bruising begin to blossom on her skin and, as his shirt slipped and exposed her, there were few places he saw that were not marked in some way. Now it was not surprising that she'd flinched as he held her close in the night.

She never stopped, in spite of the pain clear in every step she took. This Aigneis continued to walk toward the stream as he'd ordered and never once looked back or hesitated. The sun's light grew stronger with each passing minute and just before she entered the shadows of the trees he saw that her hair was silver, streaked with black.

The length of it spoke of a humiliating punishment, a public sign of the loss of status or honor, and he wondered at it. A disobedient female serf, an unfaithful wife or leman, any willful or offending woman could be dealt such punishment—a beating and the loss of her hair. The way she dealt with her pain and her uncertainty, for he could read that in her gray eyes every time he looked at her, spoke of honor and strength.

She disappeared into the trees and Breac turned back to his task, quickly gathering and packing away any items he needed. The skin of ale was nearly empty so he carried it down to the stream to fill it for their journey. When they reached the next village, he could use a few

of his coins to buy more and to buy food.

Breac pushed through the last branches before the rushing water and stopped. He thought she'd walked straight to the water's edge but her path had taken her a different way and she stood in front of him now facing the flowing stream. He watched, holding his breath as he did, as she eased his shirt off her shoulders and down. If he only saw the feminine curves of her body, narrow waist and full hips, he would have been rock-hard in an instant. But the sight before him made his stomach turn.

Not a place on her skin was unmarked.

Lash and cane marks marred her back and buttocks and legs—bruises there and every other possible place from fists or some other weapon. Though none other than the gash he'd wrapped broke the skin, these were evidence of great anger and the need to inflict as much pain as possible. She knelt down slowly and bent over to scoop some water onto her face and arms and he closed his eyes.

He'd seen discipline. Hell, he'd been the recipient of a beating or the lash more than once for disobedience to his father or to his lord, but never had he seen such treatment inflicted as this. Breac moved back as quietly as he could, determined not to add to her humiliation with his gawking. When he was free of the trees, he walked back to the two sacks of his supplies and waited for her return.

Breac thought of his choices and was not satisfied

with any of them. He could not fight her battles, whatever they were and no matter the impulse to do so, because he needed to return to his sister as soon as possible. His hand moved to the precious herbs still wrapped and packed safely with the pouch at his waist. Every delay in this journey was a risk to her survival, every hour increased the chances that she would not recover.

From the injuries he saw, Aigneis's ability to keep pace with him was not possible. Her stiff and painful gait across the clearing and down to the stream made it clear she would be a hindrance to his journey home. And though his sister teased him about his tendency to take in stray and injured animals, this was one injured creature he could not.

He also knew that if … when his sister recovered and found out that he had abandoned such a one as Aigneis, he would see disappointment in her eyes and could not bear such a thing. So, he either had to not let Fenella find out or … he needed to help Aigneis. He wavered between the choices, convincing himself one way and then the other until she walked into the clearing.

Her chin lifted as she spied him watching and she struggled to keep her steps moving smoothly. If he hadn't seen the marks and the injuries, he might even have believed what she tried to fake. When she met his gaze, he nearly stopped breathing.

Her eyes, now visible in the growing light of day, were like something otherworldly. Almost an exact

match in color to her hair, an unusual shade of silver, they seemed to reflect the sun's light back at him. And her skin …

He'd seen the places covered by his shirt and cloak, but the skin on her face seemed to glow in vibrance, making her look younger than the age he thought her to be. Aye, he'd noticed the difference in their age, with her having at least five more years than he did. In spite of that, she seemed younger now.

She walked up to him, remaining more than an arm's length away, and nodded. "I am ready."

So she was, but was he ready to begin this journey? If she could display this bravery in the face of a completely unknown future, surely he could?

With an offered prayer that she would not be a distraction from his true task at hand and that whatever caused him to intervene was not a case of scattered wits, he positioned his leather sacks over his shoulder. As he gave a final tug on the straps, he thought he heard his sister's laughter.

Without another word, he nodded back at Aigneis and began walking.

Four

It took little more than twenty paces for all his good intentions to fall apart. She could not walk at his pace, not because he was taller and had longer strides, which he did, but because her feet were bare. As he cursed himself for such obvious stupidity, he thought on how to best remedy it. She already wore his spare shirt and his cloak and he had not another pair of shoes or boots. In the end, it was Aigneis who sorted out a solution.

Soon, with the bottom of his shirt torn into strips and wrapped around her feet, they walked north away from the glen.

She never complained and never slowed unless he did, but Breac could read the exhaustion in her eyes, those luminous eyes that seemed to show her emotions. But he found himself easing the grueling pace he'd set for most of the morning and watching from the corner of his eyes for any sign she could not continue.

And cursing himself as he did.

When she stumbled for the third time, he stopped.

Wiping the sweat from his eyes with the back of his hand, he looked up at the sun and knew it was almost at its highest in the sky. There was another eight or so hours of light, another eight or so hours of walking, left in this day. One glance at Aigneis told him she could not do it. Breac handed her the skin with the last of the watered ale.

"There is a village another hour's walk from here," he said, still not certain of what he would do. "Can you make it there and we will stop for food and rest?"

She swallowed another mouthful from the skin and gave it back to him. "I will," she answered.

Not "I can," but "I will," as though sheer force of will would drive her along. And, from what he'd seen of her this last day, he was certain it would. Breac slung the skin over his shoulder and nodded, more confused about her than before.

And more confused over his path.

From her bearing and the softness of her hands, he knew she was noble. She had not worked the fields or labored as a goodwife in a croft. She had lived with others doing the work for her, yet she had been exiled. Nothing made sense to him about her.

The lust and desire he felt at times he could understand—he was a man with needs of the flesh and eyes in his head to see her womanly form. Sleeping next

to her in the night, his body reacted as it should—he woke hard and ready to couple with the woman at his side. His prick did not need to know more than that she was there.

His mind though struggled with the confusing knowledge, or lack of it, about her. The most vexing thing was his reaction to her and this fierce growing need within him to protect her. Breac must make a decision about her by the time they reached the village or he would lose too many hours today.

With at least an hour of time to think on the matter, he stood and began walking along the rough road, expecting that she would follow.

Aigneis kept her gaze on his back and took one mindless step after another along the road. She would recover, she knew she would, but each time she was injured, it took longer and longer. Every year away from the sith, her body returned back to its human frailty. And she'd noticed the biggest changes after seven years.

Her obvious health and vigor gave Donnell hopes for a child, a son, an heir to his and his father's lands and power. Though he knew it not, she believed that the ease with which she'd borne children, sons, for the sith prince would happen again with Donnell. Seven years they tried and failed and his disappointment became sharper and angrier with the passing of each year.

Part of her hoped for children, to fill the emptiness

within her for the ones she'd lost. Part of her was pleased she did not conceive when faced with Donnell's bitter anger and unfaithfulness. Then, three years ago her husband began his pursuit of a new wife and his plan to rid himself of Aigneis. The worst betrayal was her father's support for breaking the marriage contract.

Tears gathered in her eyes and she wiped them away. The sith prince had warned her about Donnell, but Aigneis did not heed the warning of what was to come if she left the sith world. Taking in a labored breath and letting it out slowly, she brought her attention back to the road … and to the man before her.

She knew he watched her as they walked, discreetly so that she would not notice, but she had. The cant of his head as he led her down the road belied his seeming inattention to her. And each step he took that did not leave her behind made her wonder more about this Breac.

Most men, nay all men, she knew would never have stepped into the situation that presented itself to him in the middle of nowhere. Facing down armed men on a mission from their lord? Saving a stranger, a woman, from a fate decreed by her rightful lord? Staying at her side with no reason to? She shook her head. This Breac was different from any man she'd ever met and part of it was some sense of his deep and abiding honor.

Even now, when his purpose, whatever it was, should take him swiftly away from her halting steps, he waited for her and adjusted his pace so she was not left behind.

Aigneis thought on his actions and the words he'd spoken in the night as they walked toward the village ahead. Fenella. Sick. Dying. The thought of this woman dying terrified Breac and tore his heart apart. Again, his honor was clear in his actions.

Thinking about him was easier than considering her own life, her own sins, and her own future, so she did that as they walked. About an hour later, he finally stopped and held out the skin to her to drink.

"Finish it. The village lies ahead and I will get more," he said as though in answer to her unspoken question. She lifted it up and drank every drop she could squeeze from it.

He took it from her. Lifting the two other sacks from his shoulder, he placed them on the ground and motioned for her to sit. "It should take me about an hour to return," he began to explain. "Stay here, out of sight, and you should be safe."

"Wait," she said, as she placed her hand on his arm. "Why are you helping me?" He startled at both her touch and her question. Then she dared to ask more. "Who is Fenella?"

He drew back quickly, stumbling over a small rock in the path behind him. Regaining his balance, his eyes took on that stark, empty expression of guilt and sorrow. "How ...?"

"You spoke her name in your sleep," she said, shocked at the extent of his sorrow. "Is she the reason for

your relentless pace?"

Aigneis thought he would answer. However, he opened and closed his mouth several times as though trying to make words come out before he turned and walked away. She thought to call out to him, to offer an apology to him, but within seconds, his long legs had carried him too far for him to hear her.

Unless she used the voice.

Not strong enough and not ready to reveal any more of herself to this stranger, she sat and watched him leave. Only when she spied his leather sacks did she feel comforted that he would return ... for them.

Taking hold of them, she carried them deeper into the shadow of the trees, found a dry spot, and lay down there. Using one sack to pillow her head, she drew his cloak tightly around her and curled up to sleep while she waited. Only through sleep could she recover her strength and, if he was going to leave her on her own, she needed that strength.

When she next opened her eyes, she found him sitting nearby watching her sleep.

Breac held out a chunk of bread to her and she sat up, untwisted the cloak from around herself, and reached out for it. He did the same with a piece of roasted fowl and a small wedge of cheese. And she ate whatever he handed her, famished from both the walking since dawn and the healing that was happening within her. She stopped only when he did and washed it down with a long drink from

a new skin of ale. Her stomach had not been full in many, many days and it felt wonderful.

"Fenella is my sister," he said without preamble. "She is ill and I must return."

"What is wrong with her?" Aigneis asked. "Has she seen a healer?" She looked around for something to wipe her hands on, but there was none. "How old is she?"

Her curiosity was rising as her strength did. 'Twas not a matter of her concern, but she was touched that he explained himself. Most men she knew … She shook her head.

"She is the reason for your haste and I delay you from her," she said, finally putting some of the bits and pieces of knowledge and observation together. Climbing to her feet, she nodded at him. "My thanks for your help and for the food."

Doubt crept into his expression now, his dark brown eyes wide and staring at her. He held out a bundle to her. Clothing it seemed.

"Get dressed. Then we can speak on this."

Aigneis took the bound pile of fabric from him and turned her back. Tugging the string free from it, she found a shift, a gown and tunic, and, more surprising, a pair of stockings and soft leather shoes. The last item was a square piece of material to cover her head. With barely a glance back to see if he watched, she dropped the cloak, shrugged off his shirt and dressed in the clean garments.

Folding the fabric into a triangle, she wrapped it

around her head, catching the wild curls under it and securing it at the nape of her neck. 'Twas not the jeweled circlet and fine linen veil she used to wear, but it covered the evidence of her shame and made her feel safe again. Aigneis turned back to face Breac and found him staring at her.

He'd seen her skin!

The look on his face, eyes widened in disbelief, spoke of his shock. The frown that followed told her he was trying to figure out what he'd seen only this morning and how it could be healed now. The shake of his head demonstrated how he could not believe it.

She waited for the next emotional step—the one that usually followed the disbelief, the shock, and the inability to understand.

Fear.

Hatred.

Anger.

Aigneis was tempted to close her eyes so she would not see his. To this point, he'd surprised her with his reactions to finding himself in the middle of something not of his making or concern. The intervention, the protection, and the way he saw to her needs were not what she was accustomed to facing. Now was the time when he would react as all other men did when faced with the reality of her.

Aigneis held her breath and waited and watched for the inevitable to happen.

Five

The bruises.

The lash and cane marks.

All nearly gone.

Had he only imagined them there and now saw the truth? Or had they disappeared in just hours?

How?

She'd moved quickly and he'd turned away to give her some measure of privacy, but not before catching a glimpse of her legs and her back. Now, instead of the angry red and purple crisscross markings of punishment, her skin was nearly unmarred, nearly perfection in its creamy whiteness. Instead of a damaged victim, a woman stood in her place.

Breac considered himself a man with some intelligence, not the wisest or most knowledgeable, but he was known for his logical thinking and common sense. That was why Lord Malcolm appointed him as

overseer to the village and consulted him on matters about the crops and supplies. Neither of those skills or that position helped now in the face of this incredible situation. When he met her gaze, he could see that she watched him and waited for some reaction.

"How?" he asked, the word escaping before he could stop it.

Part of him wanted to tear off her clothes to see if he mistook the shadows she stood in for changes to the color of her skin. Part wanted to run, run back to his village and to his sister and forget he'd met a woman such as this. But the part that won out was the man inside him who had seen the real pain and shame and fear in her gaze and the true injuries to her body and discovered that he wanted to banish both from her forever.

"How?" he asked again.

She looked away then and would not meet his eyes. Her hands twisted in his shirt and cloak which she held tightly, positioned almost as he would a weapon before him. She shrugged.

"I know not."

Aigneis may not know the whole of it, but the guilt now lacing her expression said she knew some of it. And she was not going to reveal what she did know.

He swore not to allow her to distract him from his purpose and this new aspect about her threatened his will more than anything else she'd done or said. Fenella lay dying, a certainty if he did not return with the

medicaments in his bag, a possibility even if he did return. So, even fascination and intrigue could not sway him from the decision he'd made on the way to the village.

Even fascination and intrigue wrapped in the feminine curves of this woman before him.

"I spoke with the blacksmith of the village. I know him from other dealings in the past and he is a good man."

"The blacksmith?" she stuttered.

"Aye. Once you recover …" he stumbled over the words now. "He will see you to his cousin who lives north of here and will offer you a place to live. You will be safe there while you decide about your future."

The words rushed out of him and he could see their effect on her. Like more blows raining down on her, she flinched with his attempt to separate their paths, one from the other. Then he watched her gather the shards of her pride around herself and nod in reply.

Aigneis folded the torn and dirty shirt and cloak and handed them back to him. Then she packed up the leftover food into one of the sacks and waited as he did the other. She did not say anything as he led her down the path back to the village. Her steps seemed less labored than earlier though she rarely met his gaze or said a word at all.

He tried to convince himself of the rightness of his decision. They were strangers. He'd managed to save her

life. He had his own responsibilities to which and to whom he must return as quickly as possible. She could not be part of his life.

Breac walked on, trying to use those words to convince his heart that he was making the right decision, but he knew only that his heart was not listening.

Aigneis understood his reaction—she'd seen it before, whether in her father's eyes or Donnell's or his men's or many others when faced with the strange remnants of sith left in her. Most were not as honorable as Breac though, for he made arrangements for her even though he could not or would not take her with him. And though they were strangers and he'd done more than her own family had for her, she had no claim on him or his life.

So, she would honor his actions by letting him leave without question or argument. Without begging to stay with him as her heart wanted to do. She shook her head in disbelief at the very thought of it.

Aigneis had followed her heart's desires twice in her life, and the cost turned out to be dear—first her sons to their father's curse and then her own life to her husband's needs. She would not do it again, no matter that he seemed honorable or good. It would not last when his wishes and needs exceeded hers.

And when that happened, she feared the possible cost of such a betrayal. What did she have left to lose? Her soul?

So, she kept her thoughts to herself and walked along the road behind him—more comfortable in the clothing and shoes he'd brought and in less pain than earlier, but more uncomfortable for knowing the truth of it.

He was just like the other men in her life.

'Twas hard to think of him like that when she noticed he still slowed his pace so she could keep up with him. And when he kept glancing back to make certain she was following. And especially when he waited for her so they could enter the village side-by-side and without her trailing like a serf.

Soon, within shockingly few minutes, she found herself standing at the smith's cottage, watching Breac leave her behind. Aigneis had learned how low her husband had sunk in his attempts to rid himself of an unwanted wife and how low her father had in order to keep as much of her gold as possible for his own use. But this hurt her in some way she could not describe.

She only knew she was not content to stay and let him leave. His honor demanded he get back to his sister, but there was nothing to keep her from following him. And when she remembered his frantic whispers in the night that spoke of his fears for his sister's life, Aigneis knew she wanted to be there to take the pain from his gaze and his heart when his sister did not survive.

She could not explain how she knew that, but she did. And she suspected that he did, too. So, she found herself back on the road, trying to catch up with him before the

distance became too great. An hour later, she walked along the road as it curved sharply and spied Breac coming toward her. Aigneis stopped and waited for him.

The doubts struck within minutes of leaving the village … and leaving Aigneis behind. Breac knew, he knew, it was the right thing to do, but something forced him back to get her. He did not own her, nor did he have any claim on her. He knew both of those things well. His heart whispered other things to him.

Finally, his practical part won out, deciding that he would ask her to come and care for his sister. It made sense. He would not have to worry about her care if Aigneis was there. He would not have to hire others to see to her during the days when he spent his hours at his duties for Lord Malcolm. He did not fool himself about the other reasons, the ones he did not think but felt through his flesh and bone.

He wanted her.

The vitality she offered. The curves of her body. The scent and creaminess of her skin. Everything about her tugged at him like an unseen cord, pulling him to her.

Even now, the thought of the way she felt against him in the night made him hard. The memory of the full breasts and hips that he saw as she dressed. The riotous silver curls—covered now—that begged him to pull off the kerchief and run his fingers through them. The mouth that could utter words and a name in a way that made him

feel it instead of hear it.

All that and more and the intensity of it shocked and worried him. Not usually a man to be controlled by needs of the flesh, the power of his desire for her was something new.

He'd turned and was heading back to the village before he ever made the decision. Breac did not see her until he almost walked into her as she stood by the road. Puzzled to find her there and not in the village, he noticed she carried the sack of additional clothing he'd purchased from one of the villagers for her. Her expression gave no clue as to her thoughts or feelings as she stood there watching him approach.

Her presence answered part of the request he planned to make, for she would not be here following him if she did not wish to accompany him home. Would she?

"I …," he said, pausing as he tried to put the words together for the rest.

"I …," she said at the same time, pausing as he did.

Breac laughed at the simple irony of it and she smiled.

Holy God in Heaven! When she smiled … he lost his breath and his mind at the splendor of it. Though none of her features, other than her eyes, could be called beautiful, when those did sparkle, they lit up her face with a radiance he could feel in his own heart.

"I know you are confused and have many choices to make about your life, but would you consider coming with me to care for my sister?" He blurted out the whole

question at once. Breac could not remember feeling so nervous about anything as he did over this. His stomach tightened, his mouth dried, and he held his breath as though her answer would determine his next one. "I can pay you," he added, as though it would help.

She smiled again at his offer and nodded. "You have paid me more than enough already," she whispered. "I would come and care for her, as long as you have need of me. 'Tis the least I can do for you, Breac."

His body reacted then, both to her smile and to her words and to the sound of his name on her lips, as visions of their two bodies, sleek with heat and sweat, entwined in passion, flitted through his thoughts. He could feel his thrusts into her womanly flesh, hear her cries of completion, and even taste the saltiness of her skin as they coupled. Breac cleared his throat and pushed those thoughts away. He was not asking her to be his leman, only a companion and caregiver to his sister.

"Can you walk?" he asked. "We have far to travel." His question sounded stupid even to him, but he needed to say something to banish the images of heated embraces that still threatened.

"I am feeling much stronger now," she replied. "I do not think I can keep up with your long strides, but I will try."

The silence between them as they began was companionable, and he did not try to comprehend the improvements in her condition. He just accepted them

because they could not be explained. He did need someone to help with Fenella and he sensed she would be able to help in ways he could not yet understand.

"Tell me of Fenella," she said after they'd walked for another quarter hour or so. He noticed that she kept her voice low and in one tone, but pushed away any thought of questioning her about it.

Breac felt his spirits lightened as he spoke of Fenella, her kind personality, the responsibility he had of her since their parents' death, the sweetness that everyone remembered about her, and many, many other things. When he thought he was finished, she asked about the illness and he went on. Some of the revelations were easy things to speak of, some were not, but he continued until he had no more words to use about Fenella.

Aigneis had not spoken other than to ask him more questions; the rest of the conversation had been one-sided. For the first time since she'd fallen ill, he'd spoken to someone else about his beloved sister and shared his hopes and his fears.

The miles moved by quickly and, although he slowed his pace, they made up much distance over the hours. Though clouds built in the sky, it did not rain, and Breac offered a prayer of thanks for that. If the weather held clear for another two days, he could be home.

After stopping for another meal break later that afternoon, Breac began planning for the coming night. As they moved north of the glen and further inland away

from the coast, the air grew a bit drier, giving him hope for an easy night. Watching as the sun dipped lower in the sky, he began searching for a sheltered place where they could sleep.

The road followed the path of the stream and they walked uphill as it meandered into the highlands toward the lake that would lead to his village. When the road leveled once more, he found a clearing in front of an outcropping of rocks, almost like a small cave, and decided to use it for the night. Within a short time, as the day's light faded, he'd built a fire, cleaned out their stone shelter of remnants of brush, and prepared a place to sleep within it.

Aigneis offered to set out their food, so he decided to take advantage to the closeness of the water. He'd not washed in days, not his usual custom, and his skin itched from the dampness of the rain and the dirt of the road. He took the soiled shirt she'd worn along with him and, after explaining his task to her, he headed for the stream.

Six

Aigneis watched as he strode away from the shelter. Deciding not to take out their food until he returned, she did sort through it and choose something for them to share. She noticed that one of their skins was empty, so she made up her mind to fill it before it was full dark. Following the path he had but turning uphill just as she reached the water's edge, she dipped the leather skin into the rushing water and let it fill.

She only then realized that it felt good to be needed and useful. After so many years of being made to feel like a burden to others and forced to know she was unwanted, knowing that she could help and would help, brought her a satisfaction she'd not felt in a very long time. And by the time she was not needed by Breac and his sister, her mind would sort through her choices and accept one.

Aigneis stood with the heavy skin in her hand and lost

her balance, stumbling and landing on her bottom. She managed to keep her grasp on the skin so it did not float off downstream in the water. Laughing to herself, she began to climb to her feet but the sight before her stopped her. Some yards downstream, blocked by some brush, Breac stood.

Naked.

He walked out of the bushes to the water's edge and crouched down to wash his body.

Aigneis' own body reacted to his male form by sending waves of heat then ice through her veins.

His strong arms connected to a wide muscular chest that was covered with black hair, which tapered down below his narrow waist and hips before covering his prick. His thighs were like tree trunks, even more muscular than his chest. She thought his body closer to the sith prince's, when in a human form, than to her husband's, and her entire body warmed as she thought about touching the curls on his chest and stomach and …

He turned then and she glimpsed his back. It was no less impressive than the other part of him, with each limb and back and buttocks covered in muscles that rippled as he moved. Her mouth went dry as he bent over, splashed water on his skin, and then rubbed it to clean himself. She'd felt those muscles, that strength, as he'd lifted her, held her on her feet, carried her from the stream, and then when he'd lain with her in the night.

What would it feel like to couple with such a man? To

feel his strong hands running over her skin and to have him push his hardened ...

Shaking herself free of such gawking and fleshly thoughts, she scrambled to her feet and walked back to the shelter. Her face grew heated and the place between her legs grew both heated and wet as she remembered his form, his flesh, and his strength. That heat threatened to burst into flames when he walked back from the stream wearing only his trews.

Aigneis tried not to notice the way that garment lay loose over his hips, or how his stomach rippled as he leaned forward and tossed his other wet clothes over bushes to dry. Or how his arms flexed as he reached up and tied his hair back with a thin strip of leather. He finished and approached and Aigneis realized the food was not ready!

She quickly opened a cloth on the ground and placed the roasted meat, cheese, and last chunk of bread there. He reached down for the skin she'd dropped and hefted it in his hand. She could tell the moment he noticed it was filled and then when he realized what she had done and where. The heat of embarrassment crept further into her cheeks and it was all she could do to keep from covering them with her hands.

They ate in silence, as she considered about this situation. She'd coupled with a man, well, a male, when she thought it was for love and with her husband when she knew it was for duty, but her thoughts today involved

neither of those. Donnell's disavowal of their marriage was accepted by everyone, except her, and it meant they were no longer man and wife. But Aigneis had been faithful to her vows and had given her oath to remain his wife until death.

Men of noble status always had a leman, and 'twas not unusual at all for them to couple with women other than their legal wives. Some of higher and royal status even had concubines, but women were expected to do their duty, accept their husbands' attentions, and bear his children.

She gazed across at Breac as he ate. She'd not asked him about a wife. She never thought to ask such a question of him, with his attention focused on his sister. He wanted her, 'twas clear in the way he looked at her, but would it be as leman? Would she supplant someone else in his bed? Somehow, she could not imagine him taking a mistress while married.

"Do you have a wife?" she asked. Better to know than to be surprised later.

He choked on the food in his mouth and had to cough several times to clear it and be able to breathe. "Nay," he finally said. Drinking some water, he finally felt as though he could speak. "Though once my sister is well, 'tis something that Lord Malcolm would like to see accomplished."

Breac could see her thinking on his words and wondered what she would ask next. He thought her

silence through dinner had been out of embarrassment that he knew she'd spied on him at the stream. But this question bespoke of more personal matters.

"Is your lord interested in your marriage because you are serf? Or family mayhap?" she asked as she tossed the last of her bread in her mouth and chewed it.

"Family," he answered. "Though a distant connection, I am cousin to his wife and serve him as a freeman. He would like me to marry and settle permanently with him."

Some indefinable emotion passed over her face for an instant and then it was gone. She settled back into silence as they finished their food and packed the rest away for their journey on the morrow. He never claimed to understand the way women behaved or thought, but he suspected she wondered about the coming night.

As did he.

He saw her as she ran away from the stream and knew she'd been watching him there. Her perusal since his return and through their meal included moments of plain scrutiny as well as secret glances at his body and his face. 'Twas her body's reaction that told him she thought about tupping—for each time she looked at him, a blush crept into her cheeks or her breathing grew shallow or, more telling than those, her nipples tightened into peaks he could see pressing against the gown and tunic she wore.

Breac turned his attentions back to preparing for

sleep. He banked the small fire so that it would continue to burn low for a bit longer and then took his cloak and spread it next to the fire, under the cover of the rocks. He sat down and watched her fidget with the sacks of supplies and food and the skins until she'd arranged them and rearranged them several times. Holding out his hand, he made his offer.

"Lie with me," he said softly.

The first reaction she had was that her blush grew stronger until he thought she might burst. Then, she glanced from him to the cloak and back again three times. Her question made him laugh.

"To sleep?"

"We did so last night and you came to no harm," he said.

Though his body and especially his cock clamored for more than sleeping next to her, his honor would not permit him to demand her favors. He did not force himself on women. And this woman had been forced too much already by too many men and he did not want her to count him among them and their ilk.

Aigneis walked over to him and took his hand. He assisted her as she sat, then again as she lay down next to him on the cloak. The last thing she did was to pull the kerchief from her head, freeing the mass of curls that he wanted to touch. Holding himself under control, he moved in closer to her and then drew the free edge of the cloak over both of them.

Within moments it seemed, she fell into a deep sleep, barely moving, barely breathing, as he lay behind her with his body afire with desire for more than sleep. If she were awake, she would have no doubt of it from the size and hardness of his cock, so mayhap 'twas best she slept.

But it took a long time, with much effort, for him to quiet the raging need within his body and force it to sleep. All the miles walked and sheer physical exhaustion could not compare to the enticement she offered, if she offered, and his body stood ready for any sign from her. The soft snore that escaped her though was not the sign he'd hoped for; it served to calm him down quickly.

When next he knew it, the night's darkness was full upon them and he could feel that she'd rolled away from him. Then he noticed that she watched him through eyes that seemed to glow and glimmer. The soft touch of her hand on his face surprised him, but her words shocked him to the core.

"Lie with me, Breac."

If he mistook her meaning, the way she caressed his face, touching his mouth and outlining his lips, and then sliding her hand down his jaw and neck onto his shoulder, convinced him she did not mean to sleep. Her fingers slid onto the bare skin of his chest and she swirled them in the hair there, teasing and tickling in a playful way. But once she spoke again and her voice pierced through him, he did not feel playful at all.

"Couple with me, Breac," she said in a breathy voice that spoke of desire and pleasure and need and passion.

How did she make him feel it in his blood with just words? How was it that the sound of his name on her lips drove him to madness? Her fingers now traced the edge of his trews and, with as loose as they were, she could have slipped inside to touch the length of him easily. His hips thrust forward toward her before he could decide to do it. He prayed her hand would slip inside.

She moved closer then, leaning up on her elbows and nearer to him. He struggled to control the growing beast within, but her scent and the nearness of her body let it break forth. As though she knew, she laughed softly and the throaty sexual tone made him growl in reply. And then he moved.

First he guided her hand where he wanted it to be and then he pulled the rest of her into his arms and took her mouth in a kiss that inflamed him more rather than satisfying his need. She responded by wrapping her fingers around his flesh and sliding it as he slid his tongue into her mouth and tasted her deeply. He nearly lost his breath as she slid her hand lower and touched his balls. Cupping them, she massaged the length of him and then encircled his cock with her fingers once more.

Breac drew back then, releasing her mouth and hearing her draw in a ragged breath. Before he reached over to loosen the laces of her tunic and gown, for he wanted to feel her skin against his, he paused.

"Do you do this out of obligation?" he asked, while his thoughts could still be coherent. "Is this because I saved your life?" The rational part within him did not want her gratitude and the irrational part only wanted to bury himself to the hilt in her heated flesh.

"Would it matter to you?" she asked, her voice surrounding him and making his skin heat.

"Aye." His answer an honest one, for he did not want her gratitude. He wanted her desire.

"This is for pleasure, Breac, not gratitude," she assured him. Then she leaned her head back and laughed softly, the sound of it echoing through their shelter and out into the night. "Pleasure me, Breac."

Seven

Aigneis meant it.

For once in her life, she desired a man not her love, not her husband, not someone who could claim her life or her heart, just someone with whom she could share a moment or two of pleasure. When he disclosed his plans for a wife, a burden was lifted from her, for she was neither interested nor able to be such a woman for him.

First, she was married. Though abandoned by her husband and family and expected to accept the decision, Aigneis knew she could never again take marriage vows with another man until Donnell died.

Second, she was too old for him. Protected yet from the ravages of age, Aigneis would soon show signs of her true age as the touch of the sith wore off and she became what she was—a woman of nigh onto thirty-and-five years old.

Third and worst for a man seeking a wife, she could

never bear him children. If her true age did not soon prevent it, something done by the sith prince would. Aigneis knew in her soul that she would never bear any man's children again since she had born those of the sith.

Once those matters had sorted themselves out in her thoughts, she knew that she could provide for him something he needed and would need in the coming days—a place to release his torment and grief and passion while he dealt with his sister's coming death. And in exchange she could share some moments of pleasure before she left him to the life he must have and she to whatever fate intended.

He moved quickly then and she found her garments not unlaced and loosened, but pulled as one over her head, leaving her only in her shift and stockings. Then, but a moment later, even those were gone, and she felt the heat of his skin against hers and moaned at the intensity of the feeling.

And he was only just beginning.

Aigneis smiled then as he stripped off his trews and covered her with his now-naked body. Wrapping her arms around him, she ran her hands over the strong muscles of his shoulders and back and then down farther, cupping his buttocks and holding him tightly. Instead of quickly spreading her legs and entering her as Donnell did, Breac began to ease down her body, suckling and licking her neck and shoulders and on and on until he reached her breasts.

She gasped at the touch of his mouth on the tip of one and then the other. She arched as he drew it into his mouth and teased it with his teeth and tongue. Aigneis lost control, holding his head close and urging him to do it over and over and over. He laughed now. The masculine deepness of it made her ache within for his flesh to fill hers. Still, he crept lower until she could feel the heat of his breath on her stomach.

What did he mean to do? Surely not …

She felt his large hand slip between her legs and then the touch of a calloused finger along the throbbing cleft there. Her legs opened for him and he slid one and then two fingers deep within, rubbing against a sensitive spot near the top that made her cry out in pleasure.

And still he did not enter her.

Aigneis ached inside, something tightened and tightened and she could only feel. He brushed her hands away when she tried to reach his prick, laughing again, as he relentlessly caressed her.

"Breac," she called out, infusing her words with every bit of the voice she could. "Take me, Breac. Take me," she commanded.

Whether the power of the voice or the strength of his arousal and desire, she knew not, but finally he moved into the cradle of her thighs, lifted her legs around his waist, and thrust in until he could go no deeper. Her breath rushed out at the power of his strokes and every muscle of her body from deep inside out to her skin

spasmed at the same time.

As she keened out her satisfaction, he began to take his. Slow then faster. Shallow then deep and deeper still. Even paced then without pattern. He took her breath away with the way he filled her time and time again, over and over until she found herself on the edge again and yet again. His young hard body and hungry prick would not be conquered until he wished to give in, so she opened to him, allowing him to do as he wanted and allowing her own body to respond until she'd given everything she could.

Breac must have known, for he laughed wickedly and then rocked himself deep within her, and once more, until she felt the hot release of his seed deep in her body.

Aigneis waited for him to withdraw and move away, but he remained buried inside her for some time—long enough for her breathing to return to normal and the waves and waves of pleasurable throbbing to calm within her. Breac eased from her, but held her close, turning them onto their sides and wrapping his leg around her to keep her there.

It did not take long for the relief brought by that kind of pleasure and the exhaustion that she barely held at bay to return and drag her into sleep. Held tightly in his arms, warmed by the closeness of his body and overwhelmed by the passion she'd just tasted, Aigneis fell deeply asleep.

Breac lay awake before the first glimmers of sun crossed the line of dawn. He heard the morning song of the birds in the forest around them just as the first note was sung. And he held her as she slept. For all that his body was exhausted from the miles traveled over these last five days and the release he experienced deep within her body, Breac could not find sleep.

He'd lost his mind in the night as she offered herself to him and he feared her reaction when she woke. He had taken her, and in spite of the fact she begged, nay ordered him to it, he worried about the vigorous way he'd done it. Worse, if she woke and gave him any sign of wishing to repeat it, he would plow her as deeply and as thoroughly this morn as he had last night.

He did not recognize the ravening beast that must live within him and crave fleshly pleasures, but he knew it would rouse for her at the slightest provocation. She shifted in his arms as though sensing his attention, but she did not wake.

He took advantage of her being asleep and the growing light to search her skin for the marks he knew had been there. Now, there were fewer places where he could see the remnants of bruising and they were lighter than the previous morning when he saw her skin. How had she healed in so little time?

It seemed too unbelievable, but when he considered some of the stories told of the Old Ones and the sith who'd lived down the glen from the dawn of time, he

wondered if it was too farfetched to think it linked to something Otherworldly. Even the healer whom he sought told stories about the old ways and the power of the sith.

The biggest practical question he had for her was about her past—who was she and who was the lord she'd offended. And what would she do now.

Breac watched her face as she slept and could not stop himself from reaching out and touching her hair. The curls were soft under his fingers and they made her look younger than he thought her to be. The color was different from other shades of gray he'd seen, for it glimmered when the sun's light touched it instead of being dull and colorless. When he moved his hand away, she gazed up at him.

He had so many questions to ask her, but feared she would continue to avoid answering them. Now, the morning after such a joining seemed a good time to pursue some questions.

"Is it dawn so soon?" she asked, separating from him but remaining close enough for him to feel the heat of her body, and she his.

"Nearly. The birds will begin their morning song soon," he said. One did just as he said it and he smiled. "Like that one."

"How much farther to the lake?" she asked, sitting up and searching the ground around them. She did not ask him often and did not complain at his answers.

"About eight hours traveling to reach the southern end. I need to reach it by dark, so we can take a boat in the morning," he explained. He remained as he was, unconcerned with his nakedness as she stood and began picking up the clothing that was flung in nearly every corner of their shelter. His trews, her gown and tunic, her shift and stockings.

As she walked to retrieve the garments, he examined every inch of her skin he could see. Not a sign of injury. No sign of lash or cane. Nothing. She noticed his attention and sat at his side.

"Did I imagine it then?" he asked. "Were the bruises only a trick of the light?" He reached out and touched the skin on her shoulder where a large handprint had been … and now was gone.

"No," she said with a shake of her head. "You did not imagine it." She tugged her shift over her head and into place. The gown and tunic followed.

"How does it happen? I want to understand," he offered.

"I know not how it happens, Breac. I heal. I heal quickly."

She seemed irritated by his questions. As she pulled first one then the other stocking on and tied them in place, she shrugged. "I cannot explain it."

She would not explain it, for he could read that expression in her eyes and it spoke of knowing exactly how it worked. And why it happened as well. So,

although she trusted him with her body for comfort and pleasure, she did not trust him with her past. Since they'd known each other for less than two days, it wasn't something he expected her to do.

"Can you heal others?" His first thought when she revealed even this little was of Fenella.

"Nay," she said tersely without even sparing a glance at him. Had she tried and failed? Was her exile due to that?

"How many years have you?" he asked, hoping she would answer a nonthreatening question after refusing the other.

She stood and moved away, searching for and finding the shoes he'd bought for her. Aigneis sat on a rock and tied them in place, without saying a word. Just when he thought she would not answer him, she spoke.

"How old do you think I am?"

He'd watched her walk around the sheltered area. He'd seen and touched her body, and though tempted to say as old as him, Breac knew she was older. He climbed to his feet now, pulled on his trews, and stared at her from a few paces away, searching for clues.

"I have twenty-and-five years. I think you are older."

She nodded her head in reply. Finished dressing, she began to walk away.

"How many years, Aigneis?" He followed her as she set off for the stream. "How many years?" he called out. She mumbled some number and disappeared into the

trees.

He'd heard the number, but shook his head in disbelief. Most women of that age in his village were already grandmothers. Or widowed. Or married again if they'd survived that long. Yet she survived and somehow managed to look fifteen years younger than the age she said. It could not be.

Breac decided he would ask no more questions of her. If he could not or would not accept her answers, it made no sense to pursue them. In spite of what happened between them, she would stay with him, with them, until Fenella recovered and then be on her way. He would find a wife and settle in as Lord Malcolm's overseer.

She returned from the stream and he took his turn there. After she commented that it would take her nine hours to walk what he could in eight, they ate quickly, packed up their supplies, and began walking.

Hours later, after the sun peaked and dropped from its highest point in the sky, Breac realized they would not reach the lake by nightfall. 'Twas not because of Aigneis, for she kept up his hard pace through the entire day, but just because he'd misjudged the distance he had left. Still, they should reach the lake in the morning, with time enough left in the day to reach home by dark tomorrow.

"You should go on without me, Breac," she said. Her soft voice coming from behind as he stood in the road both grieving his mistake and trying to accept it. "Surely you can reach the lake on your own."

He turned to look at her and realized she was in earnest. "And that will gain me what? I will still have to wait until morn to hire a boat." He shook his head. "And I will worry with each step about your safety and whether you will find the way there."

The admission surprised him because he'd spent the day convincing himself that there was nothing between them except a shared need for physical release. Yet he realized he spoke the truth to her. He had invited her to come home with him, so she was his responsibility and he could not abandon her now.

"I will not hold you up in the morn," she promised as she took the sacks from him to unpack their food.

They worked well together, having gotten into a pattern each time they stopped. She would set out the food, he would refill the skins from the stream. As had happened last night, she set out their bedding while he gathered wood and made a fire. Soon, in a short time, their camp was set and night was falling.

Breac watched as her eyes drifted shut for a moment and then opened widely as she fought sleep. Then again, but this time they remained closed longer before opening. Her ability to fall asleep was different from his, for he tossed and turned for a long time each night before finding rest.

"Aigneis," he whispered, trying to get her attention without startling her. He stood and put the remains of their meal back in the sack and tucked it away before

approaching her. "Aigneis? 'Tis time to sleep."

She roused long enough to take his hand and let him see her to the covered ground next to the fire. He laid down first and helped her down to lie at his side. Once settled side by side, she rolled toward him and nestled in his arms as sleep took her.

He did not sleep then, so that a few hours later when she woke from this deep rest, he was yet awake. Breac was too restless and wondered why she'd awakened.

"I would heal her if I could, Breac. I owe you that much," she said quietly. Sliding away from him, she stared at him as though willing him to something.

"I think you would," he admitted. Reaching out and touching her cheek with the back of his hand, he stroked it gently.

He did believe she would if she could.

There was a sadness in her gaze now as she met his, but she offered no words to explain that either. He climbed to his feet.

"I will be back. I need to … walk a bit," he said.

She said nothing, only watching him with those silver gray eyes as he walked toward the stream. He suspected that nothing would help him sleep this night. All he could do was to count the minutes until the sun rose and he could be on his way home.

Breac never saw her stand and follow his path.

Eight

Fenella was dead.

Aigneis shivered as she thought the words—the words, the declaration, that troubled her more as they moved closer to his village and his sister. Even if forced to it, she could not explain how she knew, but it was, she feared, the truth.

And it would destroy this good man.

His restlessness was palpable to her as he struggled through the night before the day came that would see him home. Even now, as he walked away because he could not identify the real reason for it, she could.

Once back among her family and away from the sith, Aigneis discovered she had some talents or skills. Coming with no regularity or explanation, sometimes she could see things that were not around her. At first she thought she was dreaming while awake, but later she realized that these were visions of a past or present or

future event. She could hear things—sometimes people's thoughts unspoken rang inside her head. Sometimes the truth of a matter would echo around her, clear to no one else but her.

And she healed. When she first noticed it, she had tried to use the living force that seemed to pulse through her at times to aid others, but there never seemed enough to work on any other person, only her.

It took her a long time to realize that these too were remnants, but not of her time with the sith. These were shadows of the powers the sith prince had gifted her sons with before their births and his curse. Her body must have absorbed some of it as it passed through her to them, but not enough to do anything but drive her mad.

And so she watched others around her suffer and die and fail because she knew only enough to know such power existed, but not enough to use it. As though losing her sons was not a terrible enough punishment, this too was another one given to her by the sith.

Now, she knew, she knew, that Breac's sister had already passed away and there was nothing she could say or do. And once he discovered the truth, he would blame himself for more than he was responsible for in this.

Aigneis followed him down toward the stream, realizing there was only one thing she could do to comfort him—give him release from the tension within and make him rest so that he faced the trying day alert. He would lose many nights of sleep in the coming days

to grief, but she could make this be a restful one.

She owed him that much and more for giving her a second chance to live.

Aigneis closed her eyes and took a deep breath in and released it. What she planned would be the last time she drew on such power, but she did not grieve the loss of it. Indeed, it had caused much trouble for her and she would be glad to be rid of it, and for such a good cause as this. She undressed then, tossing her clothing aside and standing in the chill night air naked. Tiny gooseflesh rose on her skin and her nipples and breasts tightened in response to the coolness around her. Raising her arms up, she faced the small sliver of crescent moon and began to sing.

Not human song, but the song of the sith.

As the sound and tones in her mixed and came forth, she chanted the old words and sent them out to Breac. Not many people could harness sith song, but she had been able to, much to the delight of the prince and the consternation of his queen. She did not truly understand whatever words she sang or how it truly happened, but her body and soul could use them to call forth pleasure or desire or more.

She used them now to call Breac to her in the night. With the power of such song, she could offer him pleasures of the flesh that would empty him of the restlessness in his soul and body and allow him rest. Though the sith prince enjoyed such pleasures, she'd

never been tempted to use this song with Donnell. Now, the pain in Breac's heart spurred her to offer it for what would be the last time.

He walked toward her now, unable to resist such a call, and she waited for him. When he stood before her, she moved around him, stroking him and touching him and preparing to comfort him and ease the coming pain. With no resistance from him to slow her efforts, she unlaced his shirt and trews and tugged them from him. Within moments, he stood as naked as she.

His body was magnificent, young and strong and in his prime, and even now it responded to the call in the song. His prick thickened and lengthened, standing forth from the nest of dark brown curls at its base. The song came from within her, swirling sounds in the air, glimmering like fireflies around them.

Aigneis reached up, standing on her toes nearly, and kissed him. His mouth was firm and hot beneath hers and soon he took over, sliding his fingers into her hair and holding her head close as he plundered her mouth. Like the movements he would make with his prick, he slipped his tongue in and out, tasting and feeling, until they were breathless.

The song still poured forth from within her.

Breac released his grasp on her and she moved down over his skin, kissing and licking his chest, suckling on his male nipples until he gasped, and then kissing her way down the rippling muscles of his stomach. She

smiled as his breathing grew ragged. She felt his hands on her head once more, his fingers flexing through her hair, massaging her scalp, while gently pushing her toward his erect flesh.

Aigneis knelt before him, bracing herself on his strong legs, and took his prick in her mouth. He whispered her name through clenched teeth as she slid down him, taking the length of him deep into her mouth and throat. Her fingers teased the sensitive sac beneath his shaft as she pulled back and slid down again, and again, until he was calling out her name into the silence of the night around them.

His moan when his release happened filled the night air and she suckled him for every drop of it. She had barely swallowed it when he took her by her arms and pulled her up and into his embrace. She laughed as he took over and spread her legs around his waist, walking to their bed. Then he knelt down, laying her on the cloak, and kissed her body the way she had his.

Aigneis's song continued as he spread her legs and, though ready once more, he leaned down to use his mouth there. Now, her cries mingled with the other sounds of the night as he kissed and licked and suckled the flesh between her legs, bringing her to release several times before stopping.

Before she could breathe again, he moved forward and filled her, thrusting his hardness in as far as he could and then out again. Her muscles spasmed and she shook

at the power of his flesh to bring her to satisfaction so quickly. Barely had the inner walls of her woman's core finished, then he began anew to torment and touch and thrust his flesh into hers, making her scream out from the pleasure.

Aigneis felt the end of the song approaching, so she changed it as he spilled into her body. She sang of oblivion and rest and his body relaxed against hers as the song ended. The last words vibrated through them as he fell asleep, still buried deep inside her body ... and her soul.

Easing him to his side, Aigneis clutched the cloak and pulled it over them. She gave into the call to oblivion and fell into a deep and dreamless sleep.

Strangely, it was she who awakened first in the morning and eased from him. Dawn's light had not yet pierced the darkness of the sky, but she could not sleep any longer. Gathering her clothes, she went to the stream, saw to her needs, and was dressed and ready to go before he showed any sign of rousing. Then, as the sounds of the coming day began around them, he opened his eyes.

"Good morrow," he said in a voice husky from sleep. His body reacted in its normal way, hardened and ready to tup. He glanced down at it and shrugged as he climbed to his feet. "I will be ready in a moment."

She'd shaken out his clothes and handed them to him on his return. Aigneis handed him a chunk of hard cheese

and the last of their ale and watched as he consumed it in moments. With everything packed and ready, she stood and waited for him to lead. He surprised her by taking her hand in his.

"I had the strangest dream," he said, staring at her as he spoke. "Did we couple in the night?"

She nodded. "Aye."

"Are you ... well?" he asked, clearing his throat.

The shadows of the shared passion remained in his memory but not the details. He must think he rode her too roughly?

"I am well, Breac," she said. "Worry not."

"Come," he said, still holding her hand. "The lake is not so far away and we can make it there in an hour or two."

They walked hand-in-hand for a ways and in silence as they headed to his village. By the end of the day, he would know the truth and suffer for it.

Aigneis searched within herself for the words of a song, for the way to begin, but could not find them. Whatever understanding had been there was gone now and she had no song left within her. Though she frequently cursed the powers she seemed to have, a sharp pang shot through her now.

Regardless of the limitations of it or her lack of understanding of it and regardless of her anger over having it at all, the song had been a link to the sith and to her sons and it was gone.

As they walked toward Breac's destiny with the truth, she wondered if she would ever find them.

She kept pace with him and they reached the southern end of the lake sooner than he thought they would. He used his coins to buy some food and hire a boat to take them north and, before nightfall, they approached his village.

She felt his anxiety as the boat came to a stop at the dock. He barely waited for the men to tie off the ropes before jumping out and lifting her over the side of the boat. Then he took her hand and led her through the village. Though many called out to him, he did not slow or stop to speak with them, or to answer the questions that she could see in their gazes about her.

Aigneis did not need the powers of the sith to read the truth in their eyes—Fenella was indeed dead. And Breac was about to discover it.

At first, he identified people and places as they passed but once they reached the edge of most of the cottages, he stopped speaking and simply walked. When she struggled to keep up with him, she released his hand and let him run as he wanted to see his sister. By the time she caught up with him, he was already entering a large cottage that stood apart from the others.

Aigneis waited outside while he went in, and noticed that others had followed them from the village. She heard Breac call out to his sister and then again before he came back out to where she stood. The tears gathering and

burning in her eyes fell on their own the moment he looked at her and realized the truth—his beloved sister was dead.

Nine

Breac stumbled as the truth struck him and he would have fallen over, but for Aigneis at his side. Even as he struggled to avoid believing that Fenella was dead, she clutched his hand and squeezed it as the villagers, many of his friends, approached. From their silence, he understood their confusion over what to say.

"Fenella?" he asked, wanting some explanation. His mother's friend Daracha, whom he left in charge of Fenella's care, walked closer and put her hand on his arm.

"I am so sorry, Breac," she said softly, her voice cracking in sorrow as she said the words he dreaded to hear. "The fever took Fenella while you were gone," she explained.

While you were gone.

Those words damned him forever. His sister who depended on him died while he was gone. Images of her

calling out for him, alone, frightened, sick, flashed in his thoughts and the pain nearly tore him apart.

"Lord Malcolm comes," Seumas, the miller, called out.

The gathering crowd stepped back to allow Lord Malcolm to approach him. When Breac would have bowed, Lord Malcolm took hold of his shoulders and held him up straight.

"Cousin," he said, embracing him before all. "Breac, your cousin Gaira sends her greetings to you in this terrible time of grief. She said to make sure you knew that she has had mass said for Fenella's soul each morn since her passing."

It should offer him some comfort, the efforts to pray for his sister's immortal soul, but in the face of losing her, it did not.

"And Gaira had her buried in the graveyard next to our chapel, in respect for your kinship."

Again, the most proper and unexpected regard for his sister's soul and burial and Breac waited for the pain or anger or something to strike, but he felt only emptiness.

"Come to see Gaira on the morrow so that she can speak to you." Lord Malcolm extended the personal invitation, again, an unexpected gesture for their kinship was not so close as to warrant such treatment. With a nod at him and to those gathered around, Lord Malcolm left them.

Daracha and Seumas and his closest friend Ceanag

approached and spoke of Fenella. The words flowed by, his grief striking so deep he could not even hear them. He knew they cared, but his mind and heart could not take it all in. He only realized that Aigneis was not at his side when he spied her standing near his cottage away from those gathered around him. Seumas's daughter spoke to him then. Beatha was close in age to Fenella and the two had been friends.

"Breac, we have our evening meal ready. Come, join us now," she invited. Seumas nodded.

"I am not hungry," he said, but they would not accept his refusal.

"Come and rest then," Daracha offered. "Go stay with Seumas. It is not good for you to be alone this night."

He turned and looked at Aigneis. She stood aside with her head lowered and shoulders slumping as though trying to disappear from view. "I am not alone," he said.

His friends turned as one and stared over at Aigneis, who still did not raise her eyes to his.

"Who is she?" asked Ceana. "Why is she with you?"

"This is Aigneis of …" They'd not really discussed what they would tell people about her before their arrival and now the moment was upon him to explain her presence. "Farigaig," he finished, naming the village where he'd tried to leave her as her origin. "She is recently widowed and comes as companion and caregiver for Fenella."

The words explained the situation but there was much

left unexplained. Now that Fenella did not need a companion or caregiver, other arrangements would be expected for this woman.

"Is she welcome in your house, Seumas?" he asked, stating clearly that she was under his sponsorship until things were settled.

"As you are," Beatha answered, taking his arm in hers and beginning to lead him back down the road to their dwelling.

He did not look back, as he let himself be led to his friend's house. Soon he found himself seated at table with a huge bowl of Beatha's stew and a steaming loaf of bread in front of him. Aigneis sat near the hearth, separate from the family, but where he could watch her. No one spoke to her or approached her throughout the meal, which proceeded quietly with an occasional mention of his sister and the recent illness that took her.

A short while later, understanding that he must face the inevitable, he thanked Seumas and his daughter for their hospitality and stood. He held out his hand to Aigneis and she accepted his help in standing, but dropped it as soon as she did. Silence filled the cottage, an uneasy one even he could tell, until they left.

She walked at his side back to his home ... his empty home. Once they reached the door, he stopped, unable to step through it knowing his sister died there. He lifted the latch and pushed it open, staring into the darkened chamber before him.

"I cannot," he began, shaking his head. "I …"

Aigneis put her hand on his arm then. "'Tis fine, Breac." Moving around him, she stepped inside and motioned to him to enter.

Mayhap it was the darkness inside or Fenella's absence or some other thing, but Breac could not enter. He shook his head. "I cannot come in there, Aigneis. I will be back later," he said as he turned and strode away.

Aigneis recognized the stark expression of loss in his eyes, sure that hers had borne the same look when she'd lost her sons. Coming at him so quickly without warning, for he had to believe his sister would live or he would not have left her side, Aigneis understood his need to be alone.

He must stand high in the regard of his lord for Lord Malcolm to attend him personally with news of his sister's death and burial. And such an invitation as was made to him spoke of the respect he held in this village. Aigneis knew all of that because, as Donnell's wife, she watched as he doled out such regard and respect to the few he believed worthy among his men and followers.

But, for now, Breac needed time to accept his loss.

She closed the door and looked around the larger chamber. Someone had left a lamp burning so she took some kindling and used the flame to light a new fire in the hearth and two other tallow lamps. This first room held a table and some stools, the hearth in the center

under an opening in the roof and a cooking area. Several trunks and a cabinet with some food supplies completed this chamber's furnishings.

Walking to the next room, she found two sleeping areas—one with a larger bed obviously for Breac and a smaller one, separated by a wooden screen where his sister must have slept. Again, several trunks lined the walls, most likely for storing their clothing and personal items. Though smaller than Donnell's main house in Ardrishaig, it was larger and more well kept than most cottages they'd passed on their way from the dock.

Unsure about whether to prepare for sleep or to wait for his return, Aigneis retrieved the sacks Breac had dropped at the door when he entered the first time looking for Fenella and unpacked the food. She hung the skins on a hook near the cooking area and put his clothing next to the pallet that must be his.

And she waited.

Several times she walked outside, peering into the darkness and listening for any sign that he was close by. Though she left the lamps burning for his return, most of the other cottages lay darkened and silent in the night.

After a few hours had passed with no sign of him, she sat on one of the stools and laid her head on her arms. Aigneis did not feel right about making herself welcome in either bed, but especially not Fenella's. And sleeping in Breac's arms on their journey here was one thing, but sharing his bed in his house was another.

The tension of this day, along with the sadness of Breac and his friends tired her and she found herself dragged into sleep. The loud knocking on the door was the next thing she heard.

Waking in a strange place confused her and it took a few moments to realize that she was in the very bed she had not chosen to sleep in—his—and someone was at the door. With no sign of Breac in his bed, she climbed out and discovered she was fully clothed and alone in the cottage. He was not in the larger chamber and not responding to the visitor's call, so she lifted the latch and pulled the door open. The older woman who'd greeted Breac stood there, with several bundles and baskets in her arms.

"Good morrow, Aigneis," she said, walking in as though this was her home. "Breac asked me to bring these to you."

"Breac?" she asked, reaching over to unburden the woman of some of the things she carried. "Where is he?"

"At work in the fields down the road," she answered, pointing with her hand in a direction once she put the basket on the table. "The harvest will begin in several weeks and he wants to be ready."

She spoke as though Breac had shared his thoughts on the matter this morn. "You spoke with him this morn then?"

"Only about the food you needed," the woman said. "I am Daracha," she explained. "A friend to Breac's

mother."

Since she knew nothing of Breac's family other than that Fenella was his sister and Lord Malcolm's wife was a distant cousin, she knew not if Breac's mother lived or had passed. Her lack of knowledge must have shown for Daracha offered, "His late mother."

Aigneis opened the bundles and looked in the baskets to find an assortment of root vegetables, flour, another sack of oats, another of barley, a jar of butter, another of cream, some eggs, and a piece of meat, though she knew not what kind. Foodstuffs enough for several meals for several days if she knew how to cook.

"The baker at the end of the lane will cook the roast and your bread if you bring it to him by noon," Daracha explained. "And he has been paid so no coin is needed." Gesturing at the empty bucket in the cooking area, she added, "The well is near the dock in the center of the village." Pointing in the other direction, she continued, "and the stream for laundry is on the other side of the village."

Aigneis nodded at each instruction, keeping track of each location given, though she knew not the first thing about cooking or laundry or the other tasks of being a goodwife. Her servants carried out those duties, putting her food before her when she was hungry, washing her clothes, and meeting her needs. The only thing she did well was sewing. And she could read, a task not many could do, whether man or woman, but one of which she

was proud.

It had only been these last few weeks when, tossed out without her belongings or any gold or other means to support herself, she faced actual hardship. Before that, she had still remained a part of Donnell's household or her father's, though forced from her rightful place at the head table.

And when she agreed to accompany Breac here to care for his sister, she thought it would be simply assisting Fenella as she recovered, not cooking and cleaning for him. Then when she realized that Fenella had passed away, she'd not considered that he would want her as housekeeper.

Daracha left as quickly as she arrived, but not without several pointed and curious looks at her and her uncovered hair, before Aigneis was left alone with food to cook and tasks to complete. She found some cheese among the baskets, and some oatcakes already made, so she ate those to break her fast before attempting anything else. She would need fresh water, so she grabbed the bucket and walked to the well.

Though she crossed the paths of several other women, none greeted her. They watched her though, without meeting her gaze or appearing to, and nothing about her was missed. Though familiar with being scrutinized by others, she was not used to being the stranger. And without further explanations or introductions by Breac, she would remain a stranger to the villagers.

After filling her bucket and carrying it back to his cottage, Aigneis decided to try to make a stew like Beatha had the night before. Without a recipe, she did what she thought would work, cutting the piece of meat, chopping some of the vegetables, tossing it all in the large pot and covering it with water. Moving it onto the cooking rack, she let it cook the rest of the day, hoping it would be ready when Breac returned.

If he returned.

Since she did not think he would ask Daracha for so much food if he did not intend to return, she felt confident he would be back this evening. So she walked around the village, learning where things were, and then waited for Breac.

Just as night began to fall in earnest, she heard his approach and opened the door. He stood talking to Seumas and two other men she did not know outside the cottage. They all nodded to her and then the three left before much time passed.

Breac turned to her and she saw exhaustion and sorrow written on his face. He walked up to the door, pausing as though still not certain he would or could enter. She stepped aside and he walked past her with barely a look.

Ten

Breac had avoided his home for as long as he could this day.

Though Aigneis probably did not remember, he'd come back in the dark of the night and carried her to his bed, after finding her bent over the table sleeping. He sat in a chair next to the bed but could not find rest himself. Before the sun rose, Breac was gone. He spent the day doing his duties, the ones he'd neglected when he left to seek help for his sister.

After seeing to the oversight of the coming harvest, he poured himself into some hard labor—felling some trees, repairing one of Lord Malcolm's barns, and moving large sacks of stored grain all in the hopes of being too tired to notice the empty place in his house. He glanced into the smaller chamber as he walked inside, an unconscious gesture, for Fenella always greeted him at the door.

Instead Aigneis stood waiting.

He'd not explained more than his initial introduction of her to his friends or even to Lady Gaira. If he was being honest, he'd not thought on her place here today. They would have to discuss it, but he had not the heart or will to think of the future. Luckily, his friends and the men who worked the fields seemed to know that he needed to focus on the work and there was little talk that did not involve the fields, the harvest, the supplies, or plans for the rotation of the fields in the spring.

But now, in the house where he did not want to be, in the silence of the coming night, he suspected there was no way to avoid it. She'd kept some lamps lit for him the night before and this night too, and as he entered, she took his cloak and hung it on a peg by the door.

"I made a stew," she said softly. "Are you hungry?" He was not, but he nodded, more to appreciate her efforts than in a need for food. "Sit then," she directed him.

She'd been almost invisible last night once they'd arrived here, head down, blending in and not speaking. And though he had liked it little, he could not muster enough strength to bring her into the conversations. Now she appeared quite at ease in his house, cooking something for his dinner, much in the way he'd seen to her needs along their journey.

"Why is your hair covered?" he asked, realizing that he preferred to see the wild curls than to see them hidden away. The kerchief that he'd removed when he'd carried

her into bed was firmly back in place.

"Married women cover their hair," she said evenly, though he noticed the hitch in her voice.

Her voice.

It was different now, in some way he could not identify. The melody that seemed to run through any words she spoke was gone now and her words sounded like … words. He walked over to her and tugged the fabric off her hair. She turned as though ready to say something but she just stared at him.

Breac reached up and ran his fingers through her curls. For a moment a vision of her on her knees before him, sucking his cock, flashed through his thoughts and his cock hardened in anticipation of it. Was that a memory from that lost night? Had that been two nights before? He remembered being unable to fall asleep and taking a walk to ease his nerves, only to fall asleep then and have such vivid dreams of them coupling and pleasuring each other through the night.

He dropped his hands and stepped away.

She did not speak, but she did not cover her hair either.

Aigneis scooped some of the stew into a wooden bowl and placed it before him. It did not look or smell like the thick, aromatic meal that Beatha fed them last evening, but she was sure it would suffice. Unwrapping the loaf of bread she'd purchased from the baker, she sat down and waited for him to begin.

He dipped his spoon into the bowl and lifted the thin broth to his mouth. She had not figured out how to thicken her stew into the tasty gravy that Beatha had. Aigneis waited as he took the mouthful of meat and turnips in and chewed it.

And chewed.

And chewed some more.

The second spoonful held only the broth, which he swallowed quickly. Then he tore off a piece of bread and chewed that. Aigneis tried hers and found the meat inedible and the broth worse than she imagined old bathwater would taste. It was so bad she fought not to spit it back into her bowl.

"'Tis horrible!" she said, waiting for him to agree.

"The bread is good," was his only response.

"I did not make the bread," she admitted.

"'Tis good."

She put her spoon down and met his gaze. "I cannot cook."

There. It was the sad and awful truth.

"No, you cannot," he agreed.

Part of her was miffed that he agreed so quickly and part was relieved that she did not have to try to hide her inability and pretend to know. He stood and left without a word of explanation. Within minutes he returned, carrying a small pot in his hand. He put it on the table and after dumping the contents of their bowls back into the large cooking pot, he divided Beatha's wonderful

stew between them. Only the slight slant of his mouth as a smile threatened told her he was not upset.

After their meal, he took care of the fire while she worried over where to sleep. But Breac never hesitated as they entered the other room, inviting her to his bed with a soft word and a warm embrace.

That night their joining was different from the other times. It should not have surprised her, but it did. He touched her gently and slowly, bringing her release, but without the wild passion that happened before. He drew out every caress and eased deep inside of her, moving at a pace that drove her mad with desire for more and for harder and for deeper.

He satisfied her several times before seeking his release and then held her close without a word between them until they both slept. In the morning when she woke, he was gone from the bed and the house.

Beatha arrived in the later morning, baskets on her arm and an offer to teach her to cook. Aigneis found out that Breac had secured her help, if Aigneis wanted to learn, and so she spent the rest of the day conquering a simple porridge dish. If Breac thought it strange to have his morning meal in the evening, he did not comment. He just ate it. The practice repeated each day for several more until Aigneis could make something resembling Beatha's stew.

Though they fell into a comfortable pattern, she knew that Breac had not yet accepted Fenella's death. Each

time they entered or left the bedchamber, she noticed the sad glance toward the other pallet. She watched in the evening as they ate, and he gazed at the door as though expecting his sister to walk through it and sit with them.

But the clearest sign to her was that he never mentioned his sister by name. The few times she'd witnessed Daracha or one of the others try to talk about Fenella, Breac either changed the matter under discussion or he left, avoiding it completely. Like a boil that festers until broken, Aigneis knew it was only a matter of time before his grief came to the surface, but she had no idea of the powerful emotions he kept controlled … until he could not any longer.

Breac found that he actually looked forward to discovering what concoction Aigneis was making for their evening meal each day. He spent the days busy enough to avoid thinking on his loss and spent the nights wrapped around or deeply inside Aigneis's supple and welcoming body, sharing a passion with her that he'd never shared with another woman. The few hours between were pleasant ones, as she became skilled in cooking with the help of Beatha's expertise and offered him meals that filled his belly and lightened his spirit.

Aigneis seemed content in their arrangement, using her time to practice the one household skill at which she was accomplished—sewing and embroidery. Uneasy

about taking Beatha's time up with teaching her to cook, she offered to sew and mend clothing for Beatha and her father. And she repaired his torn or worn-out clothing that he'd ignored for so long.

This exchange seemed to make her feel useful and ease some hurt from her life before, and he could not disguise his pleasure in having her happy.

She accepted his invitation to his bed every night and never turned from his touch or embrace. Nor did she hesitate to make her desires known and they explored the limits of pleasure in the dark of the night, never stopping until each one had a full measure of satisfaction.

His cock hardened as it did every day when he returned to his cottage and found her there. Breac smiled thinking of something he discovered last night when he took her from behind. His body readied itself for her endless sense of adventures of the flesh, and she had only to look at him to know they would not make it through any meal first.

Within minutes, and without a word of greeting exchanged, he had her pressed against the wall next to his pallet, her skirts flung up on her back, with his cock sliding between the cheeks of her butt from behind and his fingers touching her cleft from the front. Her body wept into his hands as he plundered her, rubbing some of the moisture on the sensitive puckered opening and pressing the thick head of his cock there as though he would enter it. Her moans excited him and he ached to

get inside her body and spill himself there.

Pressing his hand on the small of her back, she arched lower and his cock slid inside her tight channel, the muscles of the opening gripping every inch of his hardness. It was more intense than anything he'd felt before and he eased himself in deeper. Rubbing his fingers over her nether lips, he felt her body tighten around his. He thrust in and out, in and out, slowly until the tremors began within her. As she cried out and her channel spasmed around him, he pushed her to find her release with his fingers against the sensitive bud between those swollen lips.

In those final moments of pleasure, he leaned over her and bit her on the tender area between her neck and her shoulder with his teeth, claiming her body as his, marking her with his mouth as a stallion did a mare in heat.

It took awhile before either of them regained their senses, so complete and intense was their joining. Their breathing slowed and they fell together on the pallet in a heap of entangled limbs and bodies, waiting for their bodies and their passion to cool. She still lay unmoving several minutes later so he offered to get some ale for them.

Breac stood and climbed from the pallet, wobbling on his feet from the exertion and excitement they'd shared when he noticed that the screen separating his part of the chamber from Fenella's was gone. As he walked toward

the other room, he realized her pallet was gone as well. A coldness settled over him as he turned back to face Aigneis.

"Where is the screen? Where is Fenella's pallet?" he asked quietly. Though the words were soft, he could feel the rage building within him.

"We spend so much time in this chamber, I thought it …"

"You thought?" he interrupted. "You … thought?"

She slid off the pallet and walked nearer to him. He stepped away. "'Tis been more than a fortnight since …"

"It was not your decision to make," he yelled. "It is not your house or your place to make decisions."

Like some insanity that lay dormant and then breaks free, Breac could feel the grief and anger over his sister's death boil to the surface in him. Even the way Aigneis's face lost all its color and she flinched at his words did not ease it.

"What is my place then, Breac?" she asked, her soft tone goading him more.

"Your place is on that pallet with my cock in your mouth or between your legs or in your arse," he snarled. Even feeling his rage overflow did not stop him. "Do not think it is more than that. You warm my bed and get a place to live in return."

He pulled the door open and strode out. He could not breathe in there and his head felt like it would explode at any moment. But his heart! His heart pounded in his

chest and his blood raced through his veins. Rage heated him and pushed him on, and even knowing that his target was the wrong one did not stop him.

"The worst part of this is that we caused her death," he yelled at her. "While I was busy sniffing after you and swiving you by the side of the road each night, she lay here dying. If I had ignored you, she would still be alive," he leveled the accusation that had tormented him for weeks.

He panted then, unable to take in an even breath. Aigneis moved around him, keeping close to the wall, watching him as though afraid he would strike her. And, at that moment, and in spite of the terror he saw in her eyes, he did not know what he was capable of doing.

She flung open the door and ran from him into the night.

Breac fell to his knees and screamed out at the pain that tore through him. His sister was dead because of him and his weakness. If he'd gotten back sooner, he could have saved her. Instead, he'd sacrificed her for a stranger. His grief and his guilt surged up and he sobbed it out until he had no more tears left.

Eleven

Aigneis had never felt terror like she did at that moment. The terrible power of the guilt and grief he'd held inside exploded in a horrible flash aimed at her. And even knowing that it would happen in some way did not lessen her fear. She ran from his cottage, down the road until she could not run any farther. Then, turning into the woods, she held onto a tree for support and wept for their losses.

She'd begun to believe he was not like the other men in her life, that he could be trusted, that he would not hurt or betray her when this happened. Even understanding the power of grief, she still understood that something had changed between them in that instant, that he had expressed some grain of truth about his feelings for her, and they were not the ones she felt for him. Though she would now grieve for losing something special between them, she knew it was better to find out the truth about

him now before she fell … in love with him.

Aigneis fell to her knees as the truth sank in—it was too late for her after all. She had not learned.

She pulled her legs up and curled around them, rocking as the disclosure shocked her. There was no choice now—she must leave. But without coins, she could not support herself or find a place to live. What would she do now? How would she live? How would she ever have any hope of finding her sons now?

The night passed slowly and no matter how she thought on it, she could not find a way out. Sometime before dawn, she collapsed into a fitful sleep, unable to face the turn her life had taken.

Breac wiped his face and looked around the chamber. The door still stood open as she'd left it as she ran. He'd never done something so cowardly before as this—setting an innocent woman as his target and abusing what little faith he'd established between them.

If there was any guilt, it was his.

If there was anyone in the wrong, it was him.

Climbing to his feet, he realized that she had turned his house into a welcoming place. She had learned to cook to please him. She had taken him into her body and eased his grief without words, and she had never asked for a thing in return, not even a promise of a future.

He needed to find her and try to undo the damage he'd

wrought already. Aigneis could not go far, for she'd crept out without even her shoes. Mayhap she sought refuge with Seumas and his daughter? He would go there first and try to come up with a plan if she was not there.

Seumas knew nothing of her whereabouts but patiently answered his questions about Fenella's last days, seeming pleased that Breac finally spoke of his sister. They talked for some time and Breac explained what had happened earlier and how he'd blamed Aigneis for missing the chance to help his sister.

Armed with the correct knowledge of how and when Fenella had died, he knew he must find Aigneis. With full moon's light, he followed the road down almost a mile before finding signs of someone nearby. Then her soft snore gave her away and he discovered her curled up next to a tree, sleeping. Though this time it was not the deep sleep she usually fell into, but a fitful one in which she mumbled and cried.

Breac sat at her side, easing her against him, and waited for her to wake so he could ask for her forgiveness.

Though not warm, Aigneis awoke feeling not as cold as she thought she would after spending a night sleeping on the ground. Her back and her legs ached and she shifted around trying to get comfortable. The sun's weak light barely crept over the horizon when she finally gave up trying to sleep and forced herself to face this day.

After a brief respite during which she simply lived and enjoyed a short time of a pleasure with no promises or commitments, Aigneis knew she must face the reality of what her future would hold. And she must find a place to live.

Opening her eyes, she pushed her hair away from her face and began to stretch, moving muscles that did not want to move. That was when she realized she did not lay on the ground, but against someone. She scampered away before his identity had even become clear and she found herself facing Breac.

Easing farther away from him, she knew this was not the raging beast she'd seen the night before. Still she could not trust that he would not become that beast again.

"I am sorry," he said, in a gravelly voice.

She did not speak. When she did not, he continued. "I am sorry for making you my target when I was angry with myself," he said. "I am sorry for not listening to Seumas and Daracha and Ceanag and even Lord Malcolm when they told me I should let myself grieve for Fenella. I am sorry for being exactly like the others in your life who failed you and blamed you instead of themselves."

She gasped at his words for they were so close to her truth it frightened her. How had he known?

He held out his hand to her, but she was not certain she should take it. "Please come back," he said.

His eyes held the glint of guilt now, but she sensed it

was not about Fenella but about his treatment of her. "And her death? Do you still blame me for delaying you and causing it?" He flinched at her words and she waited for him to explain.

"Seumas told me that she died within two days of my leaving. Lord Malcolm wanted to send someone after me, but I had not told him my destination or path. Once I left here, I could not have returned in time to be with her at the end."

"Oh, Breac," she cried, crawling back to him and accepting his embrace, while wrapping him in her arms. "I am so sorry you were not there with her."

"Daracha said she never woke from her sleep. That she slipped away quietly," he whispered. "At least I can content myself that she was not alone and not in pain."

They sat quietly together for several minutes until he leaned back to look at her. "Come back with me, Aigneis."

She could hear both a request and a plea in his words and thought on them. This incident had awakened her to the dangerous feelings growing between them, ones that would not survive what he must do—choose a wife, marry, and have children. Now that he was accepting his sister's death, his lord would begin to press him to do so. And since she could never be the woman he chose and she could never stand by and watch it happen, she must find a new life before it happened.

She stood and waited for him to join her. "For now."

"For now? What does that mean?" he asked. "I know you are angry and that I terrified you, but I can promise it will not happen again."

"You did terrify me, I will admit that," she nodded. "But this just made me realize that my place is not with you and that you must choose a woman soon who will stand with you."

"Aigneis ..."

She lifted her hand and placed it over his mouth to stop him. "Make no promises, Breac."

"Come back with me?" he asked again.

Aigneis nodded and they walked back to his cottage together. Instead of leaving her to carry out his duties that day, he remained there and spent most of the day with her, rearranging the bedchamber as she'd started to do.

Their days fell back into the comfortable pattern of the last weeks, but Aigneis was ever mindful of the future that moved toward them. Breac laughed off several attempts by men in the village to negotiate betrothals with their daughters. He even managed to ignore Lord Malcolm's advice about a suitable wife, but Aigneis knew it would not be long now that he was coming to terms with the loss of his sister.

The summer ended and the harvest progressed well. Aigneis grew stronger as did their feelings for each other. He brought her to gatherings and introduced her to the villagers openly and without shame. He made no pretense of her being a housekeeper—she was his lover,

his mistress, and he showed no sign of taking a wife. But when Breac brought up the subject of marriage to her, she knew it was time.

Aigneis just could not figure out how to leave her heart and soul behind and still live.

Twelve

A servant answered Aigneis's knock and led her to the room where Lord Malcolm waited. After dismissing the woman, he gestured for her to sit and she did. In the months she'd been here, he'd never spoken to her directly, so she could not imagine what this summons to his hall meant. The fact that he waited for Breac to be away from the village did not bode well for her.

"Can I offer you some wine or some ale, Lady Aigneis?" he asked, holding out an empty cup to her.

She began to answer and then realized his address to her. She could feel the blood drain from her face as she waited for the rest.

"We met about ten years ago, my lady. I attended Lord Donnell's court to celebrate the marriage of his nephew to my cousin."

Aigneis closed her eyes, remembering the occasion but not the man before her. There had been so many there

as Donnell showed off his wealth and prestige during a wedding feast that went on for days. She opened her eyes and watched him. When he held out the cup now it was filled with wine. She took it and drank it, the first time for such a rich drink in months and months.

"I know the sad circumstances regarding your marriage," he said softly. She could not tell if he was being sarcastic or sympathetic so she continued to wait in silence for him to make his point or his demands. "Your husband believes you are dead and would not be pleased to discover you yet live. Too many complications."

"What do you want, my lord?" she asked, tiring of this game.

"I want you out of Breac's life," he said plainly.

"I am not part of his life, my lord," she explained. "I have no intentions of remaining here."

"I want to arrange a betrothal that will insure he will stay here and work the lands for me. As long as you are here, he will not allow it."

"Have you told him your wishes? He makes his own decisions without counsel from me."

"I must have these things settled. Either you leave or I will tell him the truth about the woman he thinks he loves. And that truth would ruin any chance of a life together with him when he discovers the lies and betrayals of your past, Lady."

Aigneis's stomach rolled from the heavy wine and

from the thought of the way her past could be twisted and used against her. Lord Malcolm could make it unrecognizable just as Donnell had in order to make his case of divorce against her. She would rather walk away from Breac than see the same hatred and fear in his eyes that had filled Donnell's and her father's and so many others when faced with the truth about her.

She nodded and stood, dropping the cup on the table without regard to damaging it. Her heart screamed in pain, but she would not change her mind in this.

"I can make arrangements for another place for you to live. A quiet village on my cousin's lands in the north."

He was willing to be gracious in victory and she was willing to accept it. "What do I tell him?" she asked.

"You can tell him whatever you like, it matters not to me." He turned to face her now. "Be ready in a sennight to leave," he ordered.

She shook her head. "He returns on the morrow and I will be ready to leave then," she said. The sooner the better and the less chance of changing her mind in the matter, she decided.

"Very well, then. On the morrow."

Aigneis left without another word, shocked that her legs moved so smoothly and that she didn't fall to the ground in pieces. The rest of that day and the night moved as a blur before her eyes. She sat on the stool at his table waiting for his return so that she could bring this to a close.

She heard his voice as he called out to someone down the road and the tears began to flow. Then his footsteps as he approached, the time when her body would ready itself for the passion he would bring to her. This time, her heart beat so heavily in her chest she could not breathe. When he lifted the latch, she took in a ragged breath and prepared to tear her heart and soul apart.

Breac missed her. This was the first time they'd slept apart or been apart since that night he accepted Fenella's death and he did not like it. It was more than just the pleasure they gave to each other; it felt like he'd found the other half of his heart and soul in her.

He fought to keep from running down the road to his cottage and to be the laughingstock of the men in the village for his lack of control when it came to her. But he did not care, for she had grown to be more important to him than anything or anyone else. And though she had not shared her past with him, he believed she did trust him and would open up to him soon.

Breac opened the door, wondering if she would greet him as she had two days ago when he found her naked on the table, offering him a feast he could not refuse. He laughed as he lifted the latch and entered.

Something was horribly wrong.

It took only one look at her face to know it and his stomach rolled at the sight of such desolation. Then it was gone and some horrible mask of emptiness covered

her.

"Aigneis, what is wrong?" He dropped his bag at the door and strode over to her. Taking her by the shoulders, he pulled her into his arms. She was shaking.

"I have some news," she stuttered.

"What kind of news?"

"Lord Malcolm has found me a place to live in his cousin's village. I leave today."

"Do you jest?" he asked, leaning away to watch her face as she spoke. "There is no reason to do such a thing."

"Breac, we both know that you need a wife. You said so when you invited me here—it was only until the matter of your sister was handled and then you would marry."

"The matter of my sister?" he asked, feeling as though he was being manipulated but he could not see all the strings yet.

"I am an impediment to a marriage."

"Who has told you such a thing?"

"There is not a woman in this village, or a man for that matter, who does know the true nature of our relation … involvement," she said. "And no woman will accept a betrothal while your leman lives with you."

"I offered you marriage," he said, feeling the cold emptiness open within him. What had happened to cause this?

"That was not our agreement when I came here and I beg you to accept and honor that arrangement now."

Silence filled the room and the space between them grew and grew though neither one had moved an inch. Sounds outside alerted him to the arrival of others. She flinched at the knocking yet she never looked away from him. He placed his hand on the door latch.

"I have never forced a woman to do anything she did not wish to," he said, "and I would not start now." He pulled the door open to find four of Lord Malcolm's men waiting there.

He thought she would leave without saying another word, which would be bad, but the words she did say were worse, much much worse.

"Thank you for saving my life, Breac. And thank you for teaching me that I could trust again."

And then she was gone.

"What did you say to make her leave?" Breac asked in a tone that did not carry the least bit of respect for his lord as it should.

She'd left two days ago and he finally realized he could not let her go. Whatever had happened led back to Lord Malcolm and he would find out the reason for her hasty departure. It did not take an idiot to realize that she loved him, he'd known it in his own heart for months, and to see that she was being forced to leave him. He would find out the reason and then go and get her.

Lord Malcolm had not answered yet, so he asked

again.

"She wanted to leave, Breac. I gave her the chance for a new life." He knew it had not happened that way, but it did not matter.

"I am ready to pledge myself in your service, my lord," he said. "And to expand and improve the farms in your three villages."

Lord Malcolm's face brightened, for this was exactly what he'd been negotiating with Breac to do and what Breac had resisted. "Excellent!"

"As soon as I bring Aigneis back and she accepts my offer of marriage."

"She will not marry you. 'Twas her choice."

Breac stood silently, waiting to play his true weapon. They both knew the stakes here, but only Breac knew how important Aigneis was to his happiness and the price he would pay to get her back.

"Either you accept her as my wife or I will walk away from here and the flow of gold you earn from the sales of your crops will end."

Because of drought or flood, most of the farmland for miles had not been yielding strong crops for a number of years except their lands because of Breac's knowledge of the land and his planning and management. Malcolm had become much richer for it and could become richer still if the pattern continued.

"It matters not, she will not have you," Lord Malcolm answered now, too confident in the matter.

"Then you agree?" he pressed the question.

"Aye."

With a curt nod, Breac was on his way. He'd already bribed the knowledge of her destination from one of the stewards and he could catch up with them before they reached the coast. He would catch up with them and bring her back with him.

Thirteen

This trip was made in more comfort, Lord Malcolm had provided a wagon fit for his wife's use to Aigneis. Even though two servants along with four guards kept her cared for and protected, she was more miserable than after being beaten by Donnell's men.

And it was for Breac's own good and safety … and happiness. If Donnell found out that he'd interfered in his punishment of her and saved her life, he would take his revenge against Breac and his lord with the backing of the king and his soldiers. But the worst threat was that Malcolm would tell Breac about her life, and she believed he would do just that.

She prepared herself for his anger when she told him she was leaving, but there would be no way to prepare herself for the hatred and the fear she would see if he learned about her years in the land of the sith and her lost sons. Or the rest. He could simply not understand it all

and he would hate her or grow to hate her over time.

'Twas better this way.

And she continued to tell herself that with every passing mile, hoping that she would come to believe it in time. Now, two days later, she was no closer to believing it than she had been two days before.

They would leave the mountains soon and then head north along the coast for three more days, where Aigneis would disappear forever and she would take a new name.

They came to an abrupt stop when someone called out about a block in the road ahead. But it was neither rocks nor a mudslide that halted their progress. Breac stood in the road before them. He approached the soldiers leading them and spoke with them in a low voice. They glanced back at her several times during their exchange, but she could only see him. Thrilled to see him again and terrified over what it meant, she waited until he approached her.

"You said you trusted me," he said, standing close so that no one else heard their words.

"Breac, please do not do this," she begged.

He took her by the arm, waved the soldiers and others away, and guided her back a distance where they could have some privacy.

"I need to know what you hide. What do you fear telling me? Why can you not marry me?"

She could not utter the words, so he asked again. "Please tell me, Aigneis. You owe me at least that for

saving your life."

"I cannot marry you because I am already married, Breac," she said, giving up any hopes of resisting his pleas of hearing the truth.

He gasped as she said it. "The man who ordered you lamed was your husband?"

"Aye, I was married to Lord Donnell of Ardrishaig."

"He is a powerful chieftain in the south," Breac said. She still hesitated in revealing the whole of it, but he urged her on once more. "With a new wife ..." He'd heard of the new marriage then? His expression showed his confusion.

He said she could trust him. Could she? She'd lost him already, so mayhap it was worth the risk?

"I was betrothed to Donnell when I was but a girl and was intent on marrying him until I met someone else," she began. "On my father's lands in the western isles, I fell in love with a man. I thought him a man, until his true nature was revealed to me."

"His true nature?" he asked quietly.

"A sith prince in human form, seeking a mortal lover. By the time I knew the truth I gave my pledge to him and he took me to his home."

It sounded absurd, but it was the truth. She thought he would scoff, but he nodded, accepting her words.

"It was a wondrous place, but I discovered I did not love him and wanted to return to my home and the man I should marry. When he refused, I managed to escape

but it was too late."

"Too late?" Breac frowned. "Did he catch you?"

"Aye, and at the worst possible moment. I was in labor when he found me." She paused as the feelings and fear washed over her again. "But worse than being caught was his anger at my betrayal. He cursed the bairns," she heard her voice hitch and tried to continue, but could not.

Breac took her in his arms and held her, comforting her in a way she never thought to feel again. "Hush now," he whispered.

She shook her head. "Nay, I must tell you the rest before I lose my courage." He released her but stood close.

"Because they are half sith, they have gifts, but he cursed them to lose their humanity as they use their powers. I begged him for mercy but he was too angry at me to lift the curse. I cannot tell them the truth or he will destroy us all."

"You are here, so you must have escaped?"

"He let me go after he took my sons," she whispered, the pain so deep it cut her in two. "I did not even hold them. He took them away as they were born and gave them to others to raise because he said I was not worthy."

The tears flowed then. She was unable to stop them. She'd told no one the whole story until now and had bottled up most of her guilt and grief inside. "I returned to my father along with gold, paid by the sith as the price

for my sons. That much gold convinced my father and Donnell to accept the betrothal as it was and to accept me, as damaged as I was."

"Did they know? About your sons?" he asked, taking her hand in his and entwining their fingers so she could not move too far from him. He could feel her desolation and loss and could not believe the pain she bore.

"Nay, I dared not tell anyone. I came back changed— living in their land gave me a vitality I could not explain. I did not age as usual and during the months I spent there five years had passed here. I never get sick, I ..."

"... heal quickly," he added.

"And there's more than that. I believe that I have a bit of whatever gifts or powers he gave our sons."

"You know things, do you not?" It made sense now to him. He'd suspected for some time.

"And I hear things ... and the healing. I think those are the powers he gave them too."

"How old are they?"

"If they are here, in the mortal world, they will have ten-and-three years now." He could see her thinking about them even now.

"Because of my youth and my obvious health, Donnell thought I would bear him children easily. With the gold to soften his bruised honor, we married and he set about trying to get heirs."

"It never happened?" Breac could see where this was leading. "In all these years?"

"I think my womb will not bear mortal children after bearing them for the sith," she said. He sensed that this disclosure was more painful than the others for her. "I have never shared that with anyone else, Breac."

She did trust him, but he could feel her fear. As though she waited for the worst of it.

"After seven years, he gave up. It infuriated him that I still looked so young compared to his appearance. And that I could heal and never be sick. Worse, he hated me for the powers he glimpsed within me. He turned his family and mine against me, claiming a deal with the devil prevented me from having children. He offered my father some of the gold if he did not object to me being set aside for a new wife."

"And your father agreed to this?"

Breac was gaining more insight into the terrible damage wrought to this woman by others. Everyone in her life had failed her and betrayed her. If he walked away, he would simply be another added to her list.

"Enough gold will ease the roughest of roads. So Donnell announced that due to my sins, I was barren and he divorced me. I objected but my father signed the papers. When I would not leave, he had me taken from my home. When I returned …"

"He declared you exiled, shamed you by cutting your hair, and throwing you naked into the street."

She looked away then, but not before he saw the shame in her eyes. He reached out and cupped her chin

116

in his hand, lifting her face until she met his gaze. "It is not your fault."

"Ah, but it is, Breac. I could not love the sith prince as I'd promised and he took my sons. I could not love Donnell as I'd promised and I remained barren until he banished me. Now, married and barren I have nothing to offer the man I truly love. Except ..."

He understood the conclusion she was drawing and shook his head. "But I do not wish to be free of you."

"You will as the sith power continues to fade from within me and I become the mortal woman I truly am."

"So I too will age. Would you get rid of me because my beauty or form fades?"

"You jest over something too serious. Each passing year sees me older and older. You will be saddled with an old woman if I were to stay."

"Aigneis, you are being too noble in this. I need no children. I will keep you without the vows of marriage if you will stay. I will not hate you because you are older than me. None of this is a barrier to me."

"Every man wants children, to say otherwise is a lie," she said furiously. She had been held accountable for sins and the failings of others, too, for so long, so knew no other way. "What must I do to make you see the truth between us?"

He could see it in those luminous eyes of hers—she wanted to take what he offered but the fear and the past kept her from accepting him. Then he realized that he

must offer her the same thing she offered him—freedom.

"You are right, Aigneis," he said with more than a little fear making his heart race. He could lose her forever if she didn't want to try to trust him. "I do not wish to marry you."

"You do not?" Her voice shook and her face grew pale.

"I want to keep you for a year. At the end of the year, if you are not happy and still do not trust me, you are free and I will not trouble you again."

"A year?" she asked. "Not a lifetime?"

"Aye," he nodded. "Only pledge me a year."

He knew the moment she overcame her fears and decided to give him a chance to prove himself. And he did not mind her doubts because he was sure of his love for her and hers for him, even if she was not … yet.

And Breac intended to keep her for a lifetime, no matter his bold statement. He would just prove it a year at a time until she realized it too.

Epilogue

Southwest Scotland, 1091 A.D.

He was not even certain he'd closed the door.

Breac had been traveling on Lord Malcolm's business for nigh on a sennight now and only just arrived home. Within minutes, nay seconds he thought, she stripped him of his clothes and was having her wicked way with him. Once she straddled his hips and began inching her way down his shaft, seating him deeply inside her, he cared not if the door was open or closed.

Now he was truly home where he wanted to be.

He reached up and covered her breasts with his hands, rubbing his thumbs over the nipples until they were tight buds and she moaned. Aigneis rocked her hips, creating the most wonderful friction against his cock. He could not help but to thrust deeper into her tightness.

She enjoyed being in this position and he did too, for

it freed his hands to tease and pleasure her as she mounted him. But now, after too long away, he wanted more. Before taking control, he slid his hand between the wet folds of flesh and found the small bud that would make her scream. He placed one hand on her neck and pulled her down to kiss him while he stirred her passion and rubbed that bud until it hardened as he did.

She panted against his mouth and, from the slickness between her legs and the tremors beginning deep within her, he knew she was close. Releasing her neck, he gripped her waist and rolled her under him, now able to plow her more fully. If she objected she said nothing, but only met his thrusts with a roll of her hips against his. His sac tightened and she tightened around him and then he felt his seed release and she cried out and milked him of every drop.

Breac rolled just enough not to crush her and waited to catch his breath so he could share the news with her.

"I think I will keep you for another year," he said, laughing.

"And what convinced you to do that this time?" she pushed the curls from her face and kissed him once. Once he'd mentioned that he preferred her hair shorter, she cut it herself the way he liked it.

"Your warm welcome could have been it."

"You are so shallow if a simple tupping will convince you," Aigneis teased.

He leaned up on his elbow and kissed her. "And my

performance was not enough to keep you in my bed for one more?" Before she answered, he continued. "Then I shall have to try to impress you with my news."

Their search for her sons had been unsuccessful, but they'd not stopped since she revealed their existence to him those eight years ago. With no idea of where to even begin, they went back to see the healer near Dunadd, who'd told him the story of a woman caught by the Sith and taken to his lands under the fairy hill on Mull. And now, he'd learned …

"Tell me," she whispered excitedly. He could almost hear the lost song of the sith in her voice sometimes when she spoke of her sons or the sith prince.

"A friend on Mull spoke of a young man who counsels a chieftain there. There is talk of visions and knowledge not of the mortal world."

He watched as tears gathered in her luminous gray eyes and she tried to blink them away. "Do you think it is possible? Could he be one of the three?"

"I will send someone there to learn more before we get our hopes up again."

She sighed loudly. "So, I guess I must keep you again for another year."

Breac kissed her to celebrate her declaration, her eighth since that day long ago, and to mark his hopeful news. Soon they were lost in passion again. His last thought was that one day he would tell her she was keeping him forever.

Meet Terri Brisbin

RWA RITA®-nominated, award-winning and *USA Today* best-selling author **Terri Brisbin** is a mom, a wife, grandmom(!) and a dental hygienist. Terri has sold more than 2.5 million copies of her historical and paranormal romance novels and novellas in more than 25 countries and 20 languages. Her current and upcoming historical and paranormal/fantasy romances will be published by Harlequin Historicals, PenguinRandomHouse, St. Martin's Press/Swerve and independently, too.

Connect with Terri:
Facebook: TerriBrisbin
Facebook Author Page: TerriBrisbinAuthor
Twitter: @Terri_Brisbin

TerriBrisbin.com

by Terri Brisbin

THE STORM STORIES:
A Storm of Passion
"A Storm of Love" ebook & *in* UNDONE
A Storm of Pleasure
Mistress of the Storm ∞

STAND-ALONE STORIES:
The Queen's Man
The Duchess's Next Husband
The Maid of Lorne
"Kidnapping the Laird" ebook & in MAMMOTH
BOOK OF SCOTTISH ROMANCES
"What The Duchess Wants" ebook & in
ROYAL WEDDINGS THROUGH THE AGES
"Upon A Misty Skye" in ebook & in ONCE UPON A
HAUNTED CASTLE ♦
"Across A Windswept Isle" in ebook & in FORBIDDEN
HIGHLANDS
A Traitor's Heart in BRANDYWINE BRIDES

∽◯

NOVELS OF THE STONE CIRCLES STORIES:
Rising Fire ♥
Raging Sea
Blazing Earth

A HIGHLAND FEUDING STORIES:
Stolen by the Highlander
The Highlander's Runaway Bride
Kidnapped by the Highland Rogue
Claiming His Highland Bride
A Healer for the Highlander

**** RWA RITA® Finalist!! ♥ NJRW Golden Leaf Winner!!
♦ USA TODAY Bestseller!! ∞RomReviews Best of 2011

Made in the USA
Middletown, DE
08 June 2021